tracks

Also by Diane Lee Wilson

Black Storm Comin'

Firehorse

Raven Speak

tracks

DIANE LEE WILSON

Margaret K. McElderry Books
New York London Toronto Sydney New Delhi

MARGARET K. McELDERRY BOOKS

An imprint of Simon & Schuster Children's Publishing Division

1230 Avenue of the Americas, New York, New York 10020

MARGARET K. McELDERRY BOOKS is a trademark of Simon & Schuster, Inc.

For information about special discounts for bulk purchases, please contact Simon & Schuster Special Sales at 1-866-506-1949 or business@simonandschuster.com.

The Simon & Schuster Speakers Bureau can bring authors to your live event. For more information or to book an event, contact the Simon & Schuster Speakers Bureau at 1-866-248-3049 or visit our website at www.simonspeakers.com.

Book design by Tom Daly

The text for this book is set in Rockwell.

Manufactured in the United States of America

0312 FFG

2 4 6 8 10 9 7 5 3 1

Library of Congress Cataloging-in-Publication Data

Wilson, Diane L.

Tracks / Diane Lee Wilson.—1st ed.

p. cm.

Summary: An Irish boy and a Chinese boy become friends, despite their mistrust and prejudices, while working on the Transcontinental Railroad in 1866.

ISBN 978-1-4424-2013-7 (hardcover)

ISBN 978-1-4424-2015-1 (eBook)

1. Railroads—United States—History—19th century—Juvenile fiction. [1. Railroads—History—Fiction. 2. Prejudices—Fiction. 3. Irish Americans—Fiction. 4. Chinese Americans—Fiction. 5. California—History—1850–1950—Fiction.] I. Title.

PZ7.W69059Tr 2012

[Fic]—dc23

2011021465

To Patty Campbell

Many thanks to Anita Leung, Amy Leung, Kathryn Santos (archivist, California State Railroad Museum), Wendell Huffman (curator, Nevada State Railroad Museum), Fred Campbell-Craven, and Judy Bernstein.

tracks

Prologue

The little thumbnail moon gave no light at all. A friend to the thief.

In every direction the midnight darkness stretched its arms wide, promising cover. But could it be trusted? I swallowed my breathing and listened for footsteps. Only a yawning silence.

The slight breeze, like a sigh at the end of a great effort, sent a crumpled telegram skidding past my feet. I didn't bother to pick it up. Its news was no longer new. The entire nation, in fact, knew what that telegram spelled out: *Supreme achievement completed. Greatest enterprise in the world. Country advanced one hundred years.*

Where did that leave the two of us?

As vast as the land, the night sky pitched a black canopy above, its canvas punctured by brilliant, twinkling stars. To the east was a pair of especially bright ones:

Weaver Girl and Cowboy, Ducks called them, two wandering souls separated every day of the year but one. (Ducks's given name was Chun Kwok Keung, but that sounded so much like quacking that I'd taken to calling him Ducks soon after we'd met.)

Dropping my gaze to the valley floor, I peered eastward. That's the way Ducks had gone, so that's the way we were heading. The twin black lines of the rails, crosshatched by ties, formed a ladder so long, it could probably stretch to the stars and unite those two ancient wanderers of his.

Far back in town, a horse nickered his worry through the darkness: *Are you there?* The horse standing patiently beside me, the one who had been spirited away from his companions, lifted his head and returned the call: *I'm here.*

Shh! I scolded, cupping my hand over his muzzle. I tugged on his halter and brought his head down to the crook of my shoulder, absently stroking his face. His skin felt cool beneath my fingers, the hairs well oiled and fine.

I kept stroking his face, building up the courage to carry on with what I'd already rashly begun. Somewhere inside, I knew my hand was trying to soothe me as much as Thomas, but in vain.

A horse—a normal horse, anyway—will shy when you lift a hand directly to his face. Not this one, not

Thomas. It wasn't because of the darkness, since horses can see better at night than most men; it was because he couldn't see at all. Blind, he was, and so named: Blind Thomas.

I was stealing Blind Thomas.

Like the thousand other horses who'd been measuring the rails year after year with their steadily clopping hooves—back and forth, back and forth—Thomas had been purchased and shipped in by the Central Pacific Railroad Company for their nothing like it in-the-world project: a railroad that spanned a continent. I, too, had been shipped in. Ducks had been shipped in.

But the great effort—*our* great effort—was over. The rails from the east and those from the west had been spiked together earlier in the day back at Promontory Summit. The country, all thirty-some states and more territories, was joined end to end. The labor of our backs had delivered their dream, and we had celebrated. For a day. Now men and horses were being shoved out, discarded like excess ties along the tracks.

I shifted my weight and noted the cold seeping through the soles of my boots. Having worked side by side all this time, marking the seasons, the comings and goings—the deaths—we'd stitched ourselves into a sort of family. Even Ducks had called me *di-di*, "younger brother" in his language. When, on the face of it, we couldn't be more different. When, up until three days ago, I hadn't really even liked him.

Now, more than anything in this great, big, united land, I had to find him.

One

It was two and a half years ago, near the tail end of 1866, that I'd thrown my weight into the grand enterprise. I was still only thirteen then but big for my age, as was constantly remarked, and feisty as any Irish cockerel. I was also a know-nothing, with fists that spoke before my tongue, and for that I'm apologizing.

I was rightly my father's boy, as everyone was quick to explain; he'd made me in his own image. And when he didn't come back from the war, I'd had to become him: I laced on his boots, shouldered his harness, and went to work to support Ma and the others. The best work at the time—with some of the highest wages, anyway—was building the Pacific Railroad, and those big tycoons were so shy of workers, they were paying the whole passage on a two-month journey west: a long sail from New York down the East Coast, a tramp across Panama, and then another sail up the opposite coast, along Mexico and California. I had my own reasons for wanting to leave the city, so I inked my name, Malachy Gormley, and climbed the gangplank.

If I'd had eyes at all back then, I'd have recognized the signs of danger, beginning with the train ticket handed to me that blustery November morning in Sacramento.

That ticket, a thin white square, shivered in the breeze like it was having a fit; it fairly crackled with fear. Maybe it was because the two fingers clipping it were as smooth as sausages and burnished just as red. They were middle fingers only; the other three—thumb, pointer, and pinkie—were missing, blasted, or cut away somehow. I tried not to stare.

Behind the bars of the ticket window, the man owning the two fingers grumbled. "So they's hauling up children now, is they? Heard they couldn't keep enough men on the line." He shook his head at that sad state of affairs. "Mind you keep your wits about you," he advised, and then, sharply, which made me jump, "Well? Are you takin' it?"

I snatched the ticket, careful not to touch that angry red claw of a hand. "When does the train leave?"

He jerked his whiskers toward the schedule posted behind him. "Forty-three minutes!" he barked, and waved me away.

I pinned the square of paper against my palm, which was now damp with sweat, and hurried along Front Street.

Though the sky hung gray and moody, and a fickle wind flapped papers and chased rubbish under wheels, the temperature, I thought, was mild for the time of year. Right away I could see that Sacramento was hardly at all like New York City. Sure, they both had their rivers, but here the streets seemed wider and not as crowded. People hurried but they didn't shove. Not wanting to get lost, I strolled in a strict pattern of right turns, exploring the businesses and alleys of the immediate district, regularly returning to check on the waiting locomotive.

It was a wonderment to behold, oily black trimmed in gleaming brass, and every part on it oversize: the spoke wheels, the jutting smokestack, the round eye-ball of a headlamp. Another monster, it was, like the ships I'd been on—monsters that swallowed up humans and sped them across the earth and sea. At least this would only be one day's travel and not fifty-eight. I turned on my heel, fairly jigging with excitement, and continued exploring.

It was when I was meandering along one of Sacramento's alleys, just kicking at a cork stopper and sending it flying above the puddles, that a throaty growl stopped me cold. In answer came an even more menacing one. Being the curious sort—the kind that got the cat kilt, Ma would scold—I had to have a snoop. So I sidled to the red-bricked corner and peeked around.

Three dogs ringed the rubbish from a tipped bucket. The middling one, a bulldog sort with a patchy coat the color of beer, held a mangled fish head between her teeth. I could see those teeth well because her lips were drawn back in one wicked grin. Every part of her skinny frame was tensed and at the ready; she was a fighter, all right, and I admired her at once. Her mud-splashed white paws clawed the ground as her blocky head, sunk between jutting shoulders, dared either of them to advance. I saw her mark my presence with a calculated roll of her eyes, but she didn't budge. Her chest just got big, and another challenging growl rumbled from her depths.

One of the other dogs, a muddy black one, was bigger and shaggier. The third dog's bushy tail curled over his brown back. Together they had the advantage and strutted it. Hackles rose; ragged ears flattened. Growl was exchanged for growl, and then the black dog, an explosion of matted fur, feigned a little lunge for the fish. That prompted his ally to yap furiously while edging into a better position. The bulldog swung a quarter turn, growling with more menace and working furiously to eye them both. Back and forth went the coarse utterances, building in threat until, all at once, spurred by an unseen signal, the three tangled. Snarling and snapping and earsplitting yelps ricocheted along the alley. Fur spiraled into the air and hung there like dandelion fluff. The clamor brought a couple of other dogs running toward opportunity.

In less than a minute, the bulldog was toppled onto her back and the two dogs took to savaging her, spittle flying so far as to freckle my pant leg with foam. Before I knew it, I was clapping my hands and running toward the melee. "Hoy! Git outta here! Git now!" The dogs took no notice. I rashly added a boot to the mix, sending one skittering sideways, and the other, realizing the shift in numbers, fell off directly. I stamped the ground like the dickens, and they and the newcomers scattered, though one of them left carrying the bulldog's prize.

The bulldog righted herself. Panting heavily, she watched them leave, then turned an accusing eye on me. "Look what you've done," her expression chided. And having deposited her judgment, she set off in the opposite direction, hampered by a noticeable limp.

She was hurt for certain, and yet it wasn't the pain impairing her so much as the hunger. I could see that well enough and, having known hunger in my time, I was sympathetic. Now, one thing about having signed on to work for the Central Pacific Railroad Company was that I was receiving two squares a day, and since my stomach wasn't accustomed to such bounty, I often stashed a bit of something in my pocket for the uncertainties life had a habit of delivering. This morning it had been half a cold sausage, and as I reached for it I whistled an invitation. But my whistle had the opposite effect: It sent her scampering like she'd been hit with a stick, all the while looking over her shoulder. Wouldn't do any good to chase her, so I made myself small: set one knee to the wet ground and offered the sausage in my hand.

Right off she smelled it: You could tell by the way her nose was working. But instead of galloping back to me with her tongue flapping, she plopped down on her tail with the most indignant look I'd ever seen on an animal. *You think I'm a fool?* that look said. *You think I'll take handouts from any ol' stranger? What's this gonna cost me?*

"Come along, lass," I said, chatting her up right nice, and it was a good thing no one was watching. "Come along now." I made a silly kissing sound and slathered on the flattery. "Aw, you're a pretty one, aren't you? And I'll bet you've not had your breakfast yet this morning. How about a nice bit of sausage? It's right good; I ate the other bit. There's no tea to go with it, but you're not bothered, are you?"

She let go of a sigh, all the while shifting her eyes between the sausage and me. She was calculating the odds and coming to a decision. I knew which way her insides were leaning, because a telltale ribbon of drool formed at her mouth.

While the minutes ticked by, I studied her. Even with all her awkward angles, she was handsome. Her white socks were soiled, as was her matching bib, but that gave her the air of tattered gentility, like she was a royal lady come on hard times. She was smart, too. Each time I got to the end of a sentence, she'd cock her head this way and that and wrinkle her brow, and sometimes heave another sigh, like she was giving serious consideration to my encouragements. It was like we were having a real conversation. And the whole time, her honey-colored eyes were drilling straight through me, demanding honesty.

I wanted her.

All of a sudden and just like that, I wanted her. Not once in my life had I owned a dog, but for some reason I *had* to have this one. Only problem was: Did she want me? Already I could tell she had a mind of her own, and she was using it now to size me up. Determined not to fall short, I stopped begging her and squatted there, rock solid, with my arm outstretched, as still as a graveyard statue and just as steadfast. More minutes passed and my arm began to tremble some, but I took that as a test and stayed put, staring unblinkingly into her eyes.

At last she rose and, in a string of thoughtful acts, looked to the right and to the left, took a cautious step forward, looked at me, hesitated, and—here her brow folded deeper—exhaled a nearly imperceptible whine, then took another step closer and then another and another. As daintily as any lady picking a candy from a dish, she took the sausage from my hand, looked up at me with a proper thank-you, and dropped to the ground to nibble. While she ate, she laid one paw across the other, a real white-gloved royal.

A train whistle unexpectedly shattered the moment. My train! How could time have passed so quickly? I jumped to my feet, started back up the alley, spun, and stood wavering like a sapling in a storm. I couldn't leave her. I *wouldn't* leave her! And without putting any thought into the hows and whys, I searched the rubbish for a broken piece of leather or rope, finally plucked out a fraying castoff, and knotted it around her neck.

"Come on, dog." I gave an encouraging tug on the makeshift leash. "Come on, Brina." Just like that I named her.

She looked up at me, a new awareness taking hold. I thought she was going to resist, maybe screw herself into the ground and throw a fit, but after cogitating on the change in her circumstances she rose again to her feet. Her ears hung a little flatter, and she walked with all the enthusiasm of a prisoner, which hurt. Still, she followed me—and my handouts—as I hurried for the train.

Two

The waiting cars were nearly filled with passengers. What if there wasn't room? I leaped up the steps of the first one but didn't get far: The rope leash went taut with Brina sucking to the ground in fear of the huge metal machine. Its insistent, shrieking whistle and ground-shaking rattle terrified her. I felt impatient eyes latch onto both of us.

"Come along, Brina," I ordered, dragging her by the neck onto the train. She scrambled and whined, and tangled herself in my legs. I ducked into the first seat available, and she squeezed past me toward the window, bracing her shoulder against the car's wall for comfort. Her whole body shook with her anxious panting.

I laid a hand on her head and rubbed the velvety flap of her ear with my thumb, shoving some reassurance into both of us. But I was already having second thoughts about yanking her along. Clearly, she wasn't happy.

A few tardy passengers climbed aboard, and the voices in the car grew loud. Brina's panting got stronger and stronger, and she tipped her head to hold her nose high, the way a fish in a stagnant pond does, seeking the surface and fresh air. When her anxious eyes rolled toward me, flashing their whites, I gave her my best smile: *I'm going to take care of you.*

That smile melted some as I gazed through the window, half seeing in the glass my hazy reflection—with its two eye-dots of wonder and worry—and half seeing the passing world.

Had I done right by Brina, or was this pure selfishness? Why, exactly, was I forcing her along on *my* venture?

After turning that one over in my mind for some time, I came to the conclusion that I wanted a wee taste of prosperity. Since I was setting out in the world all by myself, I wanted to make an entrance with more than just the clothes on my back. I wanted to call something mine, and a dog would do, especially a tough like Brina.

Or maybe I wanted a friend.

That took some more thinking. Probably some truth there, too. Maybe I *was* feeling a bit lonely. Maybe I *was* worrying about what this job building a railroad held for me, and could I do it.

Queer feelings went roiling around inside me. I

knew enough to clamp down on them hard. I shifted on the seat, sort of itchy and uncomfortable, and felt my knee sag against Brina's chest. Her warmth seeped into my skin, and that felt nice. We were going to be fine, just fine. But her rapid panting worked its vibrations through to my bones and kind of set them to shaking. Seems we were both afraid and trying to hide it.

To scatter such thoughts, I looked through the window. I watched people coming and going: porters toting luggage, a young man in a suit and a hurry, a group of railroad workers chatting. A ginger cat crept along a row of stacked crates, unaware that a smaller cat followed close on its tail. I saw a man scoop his son out of a pram and lift him high into the air. The infant's mouth opened in unexpected glee. And the expression that passed between father and son put me at sea again, unbalanced. I pressed my forehead against the glass and forced myself to watch and marked my breathing. *Nancy boy*, I scolded.

A barrel-shaped man with arms sprung away from his sides because of the heavy coat he was wearing struggled onto the train and flopped beside Brina and me, sending a whoosh of hair tonic and cooking oil and mildew wafting under my nose. His thick brown hair swept backward in mirrored waves of greasy comb marks. Several times he lifted and sat, fussing to find just the right position, then finally gave a satisfied sigh. When his gaze landed on Brina, his bushy eyebrows rose in appreciation. "Good-looking dog you got there," he said.

"Thank you," I answered.

Brina rolled her eyes to him, then back at me. *Friend?* she seemed to be asking. *Are you sure?*

Grunting with the exertion, he dug for something in his pocket, finally managing to retrieve a small cylinder of wrapped candy. "Necco?" He extended the roll, already opened, toward me.

Brina instantly decided on *friend* and made a leap, smudging the wrapping with her wet nose before I could yank her back. "Sorry."

To my surprise, he only chuckled and said, "You need to put a little fat on that dog. Winter's coming, you know." Well out of Brina's reach, he offered the wafers a second time.

"Yes, sir." I took the top wafer, though it was clove, and I would have much preferred the orange one that came next or, down farther, the lemon. Still, it was a rare treat to my tongue, which tingled beneath the spicy disc. "Thank you."

Brina settled a pained look upon me. What kind of a friend was I?

One of the men who had just taken the seat ahead of us twisted around to ask, "You passing out Neccos?

Haven't had one of those in a coon's age." He rested his chin on his folded elbow and grinned like an expectant child. Again to my surprise, the bushy-browed man simply extended the roll. There went my orange wafer.

The man gulped the candy while giving Brina and me the once-over. "You heading up to work the rails?" He appeared skeptical.

I slid the clove disc off my tongue. "Yes, sir."

"Where you from?"

"New York."

"Uh-uh. You can't fool me; I heard you talking. You one of them Irish?" His seatmate glanced over his shoulder to deliver his own silent examination.

I nodded, my tongue beginning to burn and my shoulders tightening in anticipation. "I was born in New York."

"You like to fight?"

That set me back. Was he wanting to start one—here? Yet my fingers twitched. Might feel good to swing a punch. Might chase away that shadowy bit of fear that was pestering me.

"'Cause your kind always do." He was almost wriggling in his seat, and I started sizing him up, the way my father taught me. He wasn't that big, his arms shorter than mine. I could land a blow first. "Get a coupla beers in you and you're runnin' through the streets howlin' at the moon like a pack of mongrels. That's true enough, now, ain't it?" He looked to his seatmate for agreement but didn't receive any encouragement. "It ain't civilized fightin', the way you all do it—not a real boxing match— but I could whup ya." He glanced at Brina and sneered. "I could whup ya both."

The man's friend took that opportunity to clap him on the shoulder. "Come on, George. Turn around. You had your share of brawling last night."

"No, I don't want to." He slapped the hand away. "I'm tired of all these dang Micks coming over here with their squalling brats—and they always got a passel of 'em, don't tell me they don't—and pissing in our streets and taking our jobs. It ain't right." He shoved his leering face over the seat, so close that I could smell the whiskey on his breath. "Why don't you go back to I-ra-land?"

My fists clenched as my lungs started filling with air. But the whistle blew, shrill and loud, like the boxing umpire hollering "time!" and almost immediately the train jerked into movement, knocking me backward. Brina scrambled, and I relaxed one fist to scratch her neck, making sure to lock on the man's pig-eyed stare without blinking. "Turn around, George," his friend repeated. "Now."

The minutes slowed to a crawl and the world got small, as it always does when it comes down to survival, to battling for the human right to keep on breathing. As the train began moving us toward our many destinations, I heard the blood rushing in my head, smelled the sweat on passengers' bodies, tasted the sourness rising from my own belly. I got fired up and I got calm, focused. *Go ahead*, I challenged wordlessly, continuing to stare straight at him. *I'm more than ready.*

That was all it took. I saw the doubt color his eyes, saw him shrink just a bit, unnoticeable to anyone but me, I'm sure. He made an outward show of giving a loud snort and dismissing me with a wave of his hand. Not worth his trouble. But he took his time resettling in his seat and kept reaching up to rub the back of his neck because he knew—*just knew*—that I'd drawn a bead on him.

An icy tingle swept through my veins as my heart banged against my chest. I swallowed the crumbling wafer and looked down, relieved by the victory. All right. I could defend myself. I was my father's son.

But then, and this was strange, instead of seeing my own hands in my lap, I got a vision of the ticket seller's hands, the ones with the fingers blasted away. That tingle in my veins chugged to a cold halt. How would I defend myself if my fingers got blasted away? Even the great Dan Donnelly, blessed legend of Ireland, couldn't have fought with his fingers blasted away, no matter how long his arms.

Just what sorts of dangers waited up there at the end of the railroad?

Without a word, the man sitting beside me offered the Neccos again, along with the sort of tender gaze I'd seen only in my ma's eyes. That was aggravating. I didn't need anyone's sympathy. I took the top disc, the lemon one, and nodded my thanks. But it wasn't nearly as sweet as I had remembered. I looked out the window, thumbed Brina's ear, and thought about what I was doing.

Three

The man in Sacramento had said it was ninety-two miles out to the little mountain town of Cisco. Hard to believe we were going to travel that many miles in less than a day! Like most of the others in the car, I perched at the edge of my seat once we got going, because I had one cheek pressed flat to the window to see what was coming.

Brina, on the other hand, was fighting a losing battle to stay awake and had balanced her jaw on my knee. She blinked and yawned, her pink tongue curling around her muzzle like a wet leaf. Occasionally she looked up at me for reassurance, then blinked some more. Finally giving in, she sank to the floor and curled up at my feet, her chin secure on my boot. I stroked her fur absently, entranced by the ever-changing spectacle framed within my window.

For a while the rushing scenery was an inviting expanse of grass-covered valley baked to an autumnal gold, and we rolled along smoothly. But bit by bit my insides shifted. An unseen force pushed me back into my seat as the locomotive began chugging with more determination. It seemed we were climbing away from the earth.

I felt like a genie on a flying carpet then, because as we picked up speed we traveled above the land and below it, skirting over gullies and tunneling through solid rock. The man-made wonders piled one upon the other, and between each town lay yet another: a chiseled passage so narrow you held your breath until the car squeezed through or a shallow gorge dammed with the soil of ten thousand wheelbarrows. But surpassing them all were the trestles—man alive, the trestles! Wildly impossible, they were. Time and again we trusted our lives to a scaffold of toothpicks and this metal monster rumbling across them. The trestle at Newcastle, in particular, sent some children screeching in wide-eyed terror. Some of the women even, catching sight of the ambitious aerial feat, shut their eyes and moved their lips in prayer. There were fools among us, of course, who looked down and marveled at the height, at the sheer audacity of it all. Me? I was curious, as usual, but when my hesitant peek shot down,

down, and down, meeting nothing but air, I settled back against my seat and left the looking to others.

The scenery continued to change its costumes. It proceeded from grassland to hill and valley, then to bolder hills, and soon enough I saw this was a hard land we were entering, a world of coarse-cut mountains and rock-strewn drop-offs. Vistas and gulches. A world of up and down, and these twin iron rails we clung to had been hammered onto the earth's backbone wherever they could fit without falling off into a gulley or rockslide or rushing river.

Twists and turns slowed our progress but at each new climb the engine strained to pull us up the heights, and I felt myself straining with it. Seemed that if I didn't, we might lose our momentum and go whooshing backward all the way to Sacramento. There were times when it felt like I was a child hanging at the tippy top of a swing, at that one moment when you're suspended face-first in the air and hovering without wings. My insides sort of hung in the air like that, expectant, and it was tiring work to make sure we didn't fall back. Before long, I was as exhausted as Brina, even though she wasn't working as hard as I was to keep the train going and, in fact, slept soundly.

We were well into the mountains now, and the spectacular, brilliantly painted scenery on both sides of the train kept everyone in high spirits. Chatter crowded the car. The smaller ones, ignoring the knees of strangers even, ran from window to window to ooh and aah at the splendors. Since I was no child, I only turned my head to look out the opposite windows as well as my own, and kept my oohs and aahs to myself.

I'd not been much of a student in the time that I'd gone to school, and I'd certainly never taken to poetry, but in gazing at the outsize beauty spread in every direction I got an inkling of what drove a man to speak in perfumed words.

Brina lifted her head off my boot at that moment to give me a solemn look, and I felt my cheeks grow hot. She couldn't know my thoughts, of course, but still I put a stopper on that bottle.

We braked to a halt at several towns on our climb, more passengers getting off than getting on. Shortly thereafter we'd lurch forward and return to chugging toward the skies. Bits of ash and the occasional orange ember swept past the windows.

After a while, the rumble and sway got to swishing stomachs, at least it did mine, and I gritted my teeth against the queasiness fingering my throat. Luckily, the mountain air delivered a bracing tonic. Clean and cold, like an ice shaving on your tongue, it was laced with the astringent scent of pine trees. Welcome to the wilderness, the wind hailed, though a keen ear would have heeded the scornful laugh underlying its whistle.

Four

It was midafternoon by the time we pulled into Cisco, and Brina and I jostled our way down the aisle with everyone else and out into the breezy sunshine. The man who'd been itching to start a fight unexpectedly did a little shuffle step before giving me a hard shove. "Anytime, Mick."

I saw red, instantly and everywhere! Before I could take a swing, though, the Necco man grabbed my arm and wrangled me away. "Not worth your hide, son," he cautioned, though what did he know about how I valued my own hide? I was so boiling mad, struggling to get at that George fellow, who was braying like a donkey at my being pulled away from him, that some time passed before the man would release his grip on me. George, by then, was nowhere in sight.

"Do you have any family here in Cisco?" he asked. "Any friends?"

He said it with fatherly concern, though in a gentler manner than I'd ever known. I shook my head.

"Well, you've got a lot of gravel in your gut, so I'm not going to lose sleep over you. But a word of warning: This isn't the city. Mind your temper and be careful." He handed me the opened roll of candies and, with an understanding smile and a good-bye nod, struck out for the cluster of buildings along the town's main thoroughfare.

I drank in a lungful of the frigid mountain air, shook off a shiver, and then went exploring with Brina. Didn't take long to get our bearings, because Cisco was little more than a hodgepodge of steep-roofed buildings clinging to the mountainside, some teetering on stilts. Looked as if it had been hammered together overnight. And while stacks of firewood rose from the snowdrifts in every yard, the forest hemmed the invasion on all sides, waiting to reclaim its territory.

When we were climbing back up the main street, a thunderous boom from farther up the mountain pounded the sky. I felt its reverberations travel right through me, and the sheer power of it made me grin. Another boom ripped the air. My chest expanded. This was an exciting place!

The pungent fragrance of newly sawn wood that emanated from Cisco's every pore tickled my nose. The clouds of smoke belching from warmed hearths and fire-hot engines stirred my blood. I began to notice the way people moved along the street, their windburned faces tipped skyward, seeking the dramatic curtain of mountains that curved around them. In their darkened pupils I saw a mirroring of my own exploding excitement, in their vaporous breaths, a similar readiness to meet any challenge.

A tingling surged down my arm like the spark on a fuse. It flamed in my empty palms. I, too, turned to face the mountains. *Hand me a tool, any tool!* I had to be part of this great effort, this joining of sinew and muscle and bone that dared to hurl itself against such an immense and impassive bulwark. We were only humans—ants, maybe—in comparison, but we were united in a swarm and intoxicated with a dream. We were ready. I was ready. Bring me my hammer!

Another explosion, and this time I saw a puff of white cloud drift above the distant trees. The heart of the action. *How do I get there?*

The leash went taut, yanking me into the moment. Brina was scrambling away from a rumbling wagon, its harnessed ox brandishing his horns. I reeled her to safety. Stroking her head, I searched the street for the railroad's hiring office.

"Mr. Strobridge!" a man near me shouted. He

was waving frantically, and I turned to see a rider on a lathered horse swinging his gaze left and right like a weathervane, seeking the caller. A black patch covered one of the rider's eyes, and as he weaved through traffic, coming closer and closer, that funereal bandage served to dampen my fire some. My mind matched it to the mangled hand of the ticket seller in Sacramento, and that sounded an instant alarm. *Explosions eat through more than rocks and trees,* came the warning. *They gouge out eyes and chew off fingers. Railroad building is not child's play.* A ratlike scurrying of fear traced my insides.

"Mr. Strobridge!" the man called again. "Over here!"

Screwing his face into a scowl, Mr. Strobridge kicked his horse toward where we stood. He rode right up to the man who had hailed him, a worried-looking sort who was juggling sheaves of paper and a couple of rolled maps. Mr. Strobridge crowded so close, in fact, that one paper tube skimmed a gob of lather from the horse's chest.

"Confound it!" Mr. Strobridge spat. "I've not got a lick of effort from those bloody beggars Frank sent me! We've made not a hundred yards today, and there's weather coming." Abruptly, he swung out of the saddle, still towering over everyone by a full head. Ill temper poured from him like sweat.

A sound-minded person would have taken heed

and stepped away, but I sidled closer. Couldn't help myself. It was his voice: Irish, the sound of family.

He jabbed his finger on the man's clipboard. "Tell Frank to get me more men, men who aren't afraid to bend their backs. I don't give a fiddler's fart where he finds them. And spikes, too. There's more rails than spikes at the head now, and if I find out who's responsible for that oversight, I'll string him up." His short red beard jerked with each order and the pickax handle secured at his waist bobbed with an eagerness to enforce those orders. "Where are the elevations ye promised me yesterday? Do ye have them?"

"Yes, sir, they're here. Just a minute while I . . ." The man began fumbling with his papers, but Mr. Strobridge reached in and grabbed a sheaf for himself.

"We're losing money by the minute, do ye understand? If we don't get inside the tunnel before the snows, this whole operation shuts down."

"Yes, sir."

"Where is Frank?"

"Overseeing a problem with the blasting."

"Well, tell him to get me more men first thing, Chinamen if he has to. Throw a net over them in San Francisco. They're near as good as the white laborers, and they don't cost as much."

"Yes, sir."

Whether it was his voice, his towering height, or that some people by their very nature can't be ignored, Mr. Strobridge captured the townspeople's attention like a teacher in a classroom. Up and down the street, conversations halted as his voice boomed over them. Men shifted their eyes toward every fervent outburst, noted each threatening gesture. Even Mr. Strobridge's tired horse gave up rubbing his cheek against a foreleg to prick his ears at the man, lest he suffer a blow for not paying attention.

As the bellowing continued, I noted several men idling at a storefront across the street: toughs, by their swagger. They wiped at leathery faces, burnished a hot-poker red, with sun-rotted shirtsleeves; they repositioned hats that had wilted under rain and fog and snow. Beneath the droopy brims of those hats poked hanks of hair, variously bushy or scraggly but generally uncombed and untamed.

They, too, were watching Mr. Strobridge vent his temper on the poor map holder, but like overgrown hooligans in the back of the classroom, they watched with confederate smirks. Wasn't long before one of them began mocking Mr. Strobridge's tantrum. That spread like disease, and next thing you knew a couple of the more animated fellows were pantomiming his gestures as quickly as he made them. Passersby began to split their attention between the two shows. The hooligans were making such a racket, I was surprised Mr. Strobridge didn't call them out.

The most exuberant character, a freckly sort with a corn yellow mustache, bent to whisper to one of his mates. Covering one eye, he began chasing them back and forth, lashing them with an invisible stick. They howled and danced in pretend agony, and onlookers laughed. But not until someone up the street hooted like an owl and pointed did Mr. Strobridge take notice. He left off his tirade to unleash a bull's-eye glare at the would-be actors. That sent them scampering away, shoving each other and giggling. I laughed.

Mistake.

Mr. Strobridge whipped his head around, and that black eye patch of his blotted out the sun. I'm not kidding. Filled the whole sky with black. "Laugh again," he said, "and it'll be a sad day for your mother." For what seemed an eternity, he pinned me under his glare. I heard Brina growl, but he took no notice, just spun his head away at last and returned his attention to the unfurled papers.

I was left blinking, stunned by my own misjudgment. Like the time back in my neighborhood when I'd poked fun at a drunkard who'd tripped over his own feet. I'd lost a couple of teeth and some memory for that one.

Brina stood watching the man, her hackles raised, but as the moment passed and he paid us no more attention, they smoothed. She backed up a few steps, shook herself, and rolled her eyes up at me. As plain as day her expression said, *We shouldn't be here.*

Five

After my run-in with Mr. Strobridge, I tried to blend in with the others in town, though dragging a dog at my side brought some looks. Brina and I found our way to the railroad's hiring office, where a sea of leathery necks and mud-stained coats already crowded the steps leading up to its doorway. An official stood at the top, conferring with two others. By luck, or the lack of it, I found myself jostled again right up behind the two men from the train, the itching-to-fight George and his more subdued friend.

The friend, I noticed, was gazing steadily into the distance, entranced by something he saw across the foothills, and soon enough he elbowed George. "What do you make of that?" he murmured. "Up there. Catty-corner from those three pines and below the white V."

I couldn't help following his sight line, though I didn't see anything unusual. A lustful smile, however, lit

George's face. "Why, I think that ol' girl might be hiding some gold 'neath her skirts." He glanced to his left and then to his right—forgetting to look behind him—to see if anyone had heard, then whispered in his friend's ear, "Whaddya say we give this railroad work a coupla days and, if it don't suit, we light outta here and go sort us a little rock?"

His friend, still focused on the distant mountain face, patted his pack. "Got my lucky pan right here."

Gold? Who hadn't heard tales of the gold mines in California, of overnight fortunes? If there was gold nearby, I could certainly find it as well as them, and it would be a sight easier than railroad labor. Already, in fact, a golden nugget the size of an egg beckoned within my imagination; it was partially hidden among the rocks of a streambed, waiting to be spotted by me alone and—

A murmur and sudden hush tugged me from my daydreams of instant wealth. Everyone had stopped talking to watch a hundred or so Chinamen go marching past.

They were, I have to say, the oddest lot I'd ever laid eyes on. Looked like a bunch of girls with their long braids dangling behind narrow shoulders, their pajamas flopping around their short legs, and, instead of hats, straw baskets fitted upside down on their heads. With their picks and shovels they trudged along without a sound—most of them, anyway—holding their flat faces in one identical, secretive grimace. Here and there, though, a smattering of high-pitched phrases erupted, as nonsensical as the cackling of hens, and in reply came a brief torrent of equally unintelligible garble.

George spoke under his breath. "Well, ain't it the Ladies Aid Society. I hope the railroad ain't planning on having 'em bunk with us. 'Cause I'll march myself right off this mountain before I'll share a roof with a dang coolie."

"Not to worry," his friend replied. "I heard they keep to their own camps pretty much, even eat their own food: peculiar fixings shipped over from their home country. Railroad makes them buy it, though. Our grub's included."

"Good," George said. He gave an exaggerated shiver. "Them little pigtailed folk just give me a case of the allovers."

Striding along near the end of the group came one Chinaman who was slightly taller, though even saying that was a stretch, because he'd still have to stand on a book to make five feet in height. He had on the pajama pants too, and a padded blue coat, but above his collar peeked a patterned yellow scarf, and on his head perched a brown felt hat (new-bought, judging by its crisp brim) that was cocked at a jaunty angle.

Yet it wasn't his clothes that attracted attention; it was

that, as he walked, he balanced his pick on the flat of his palm. He was smiling slightly, all the while watching the unsteady tool like a hawk. The curved iron head rocked like the hull of a boat, and the wooden handle swayed like a ship's mast, but he kept it afloat. And in such a fashion that prankster sailed right past us.

"All right, all right. I need a dozen men on rails," called the man at the top of the stairs, and we returned our attention to earning some pay. "Step up, the biggest of you." Pride carried us forward, no matter the size. "You, you, you . . ." He began assembling the stoutest shoulders and backs, and when he had his twelve, said, "Follow Mr. Pierce here. He'll get you started. Only a thousand miles of rail to go, men! Oh, and a hill or two." Laughter rippled through the crowd.

You had to have humor for this undertaking, because in God's name what else could you do? The whole venture was a drunkard's dream, a folly, like wading into the Atlantic and saying you were going to swim back to Ireland. Well, the drunkards were paying, so I was ready to start swimming. I and the other Irish I began to see and hear around me. We'd show them the sort of grit the Irish were made of.

"The rest of you, teams of two, please! Choose your shovels and picks from that car over there." Without lifting his eyes from his clipboard, he pointed. "And follow our good Mr. Whitney here to the head of the line." He looked up and grinned. "So to speak."

Men began partnering up right away, and I cast a hopeful gaze around. But not a one was giving me a second glance. All right, I'd just march behind and shovel alone. Let Mr. Whitney see who moved dirt the fastest. "Come along, lass," I said to Brina.

The supply car, it turned out, was a rolling general store, stacked to its roof with barrels and bags, winches and rope, and tub upon tub of nails, new wagon wheels and harnesses, and hundreds of gleaming sledges, picks, and shovels. Felt almost like Christmas to reach in and close your hand on a smooth, new tool. Enthusiastic whoops flashed across suddenly boyish faces. I pushed my way forward to grab a shovel.

"Whoa, there. What's your name?" A pug-nosed, balding man was writing down the names of the workers.

"Malachy Gormley."

Something in my response made him lift his head for a closer look. He squinted. "Just how old are you, Mr. Malachy Gormley?"

"Sixteen." I forced myself to hold his gaze. "Sir."

He looked me up and down and snorted. As he finished scribbling on his sheet he muttered, "Is that the first lie you've told today?" Not waiting for a reply, he looked past me to ask brusquely, "Where's your partner?"

I twitched my shoulders, giving a sort of shrug, and kept my glance no higher than the kneecaps of the men near me. Surely someone would step forward.

"Anybody looking to partner with this young'un?" The absolute silence slapped my face red, and the man motioned me out of line. "Step over here, then, Mack, and wait a minute. We've got to work it in teams."

And he continued taking down the names of the men, making note of their tools, and sending them off after Mr. Whitney. The wintry sun had turned surprisingly warm by that time, but that wasn't what was flushing my face.

I stood there shifting my feet impatiently and watching the town of Cisco freshen with this arrival of new blood. Residents swung their arms with more vigor; oxen leaned into their harness with renewed effort; rivulets of melting snow burbled cheerily; even the horses added some snap to their trot.

From deep among the workers following Mr. Whitney rose a single voice with the first words to an exuberant melody: "I got a gal and you got none, little Liza Jane." The volley was picked up by another and tossed back: "Circle round me like the sun, little Liza Jane."

All across town, infectious smiles jumped from face to face, from citizen to foreman to laborer alike, born from the camaraderie of men engaged in a single cause. The infection lit me, too, and I chafed to get unstuck from this

spot and to throw my back into something important.

Footsteps slapped the mud, and the overseer who had been accompanying the Chinamen came loping back. "Forgot to tell you," he said to the pug-nosed man while trying to catch his breath. "I need a body to unload their provisions from San Francisco, and then I need him to deliver the tea. I lost O'Brien to the drink last night."

"Got just the body right here," a voice boomed, and I nearly jumped out of my skin. Turned to find Mr. Strobridge hitching his thumb directly at me.

"Good enough," the overseer answered. "Thank you, Mr. Strobridge." And he loped back to rejoin his Chinese crew.

The towering man in his dark suit of clothes and fearsome black patch spoke to the pug-nosed man with the clipboard. "See that he does it. At half wages."

Six

"Deliver the tea" could have been a special railroad term; it could have been, but it wasn't. Because after unloading the most stomach-twisting assortment of tinned and preserved foods (mushrooms, dried oysters, salted cabbage, and a variety of limp weeds I didn't even try to recognize) for "them," the Chinamen, I found myself performing my own balancing act.

Lowered to the status of pack animal, I'd been instructed by a squinty-eyed Chinaman cook to carry tea out to where his fellow countrymen labored. So here I was, walking slowly alongside the rails, mindful of each step, with a long wooden pole pressing its weight into my shoulder. At each end of the pole, fore and aft, swayed a heavy bucket of tea. I thought about swinging my head, like the oxen back in town, but the buckets' rhythmic swaying sent the tea sloshing beneath their lids, and the sloshing tugged the pole up and down, and the bobbing threatened to pull me off my feet. So all I could think about was just walking straight.

Brina, necessarily freed of her leash, trotted in eyesight of me, zigzagging through the tree stumps and drinking in smells that made her tail wag nonstop.

As I passed some men fastening a chain to a downed log I caught the eye of one individual who'd refused to pair up with me. I was certain I spied a smirk, and my face burned. Brina conveniently buried her nose beneath the leaf litter.

I'd been told to carry the buckets of tea out to where a group of Chinese laborers were adding ballast to the newly laid rails. It seemed that most of them were on the opposite side of the tracks, so I began climbing the sloping bed, jamming my feet sideways—one careful step at a time—into the loose, heavily clumped soil to maintain my balance. At each footfall the wildly sloshing tea undulated the long pole, and I fought to control its movement. Sweat dampened my neck as I made it to the top and began negotiating the fretwork of wood ties and iron rails. The cacophony of the labor—hammer and crunch and squeal and thud—seemed to vibrate the mountain air. So hard was I concentrating that I didn't notice the horse and cart coming down the tracks. And the horse didn't see me.

Too late I heard the iron shoes crunching the gravel, steady and deliberate, the nostrils fluttering and roaring in rhythm. Off balance, I only caught a glimpse of the sweat-streaked face of a black horse, though for some reason I noted the dirt caking his broad back. Like a machine, the large animal marched unblinkingly, and in fact was nearly upon me.

The tea sloshed threateningly, but at the last instant I spun the pole sideways, swinging the heavy pails out of the way.

"Hey, there! You! Mind Blind Thomas!"

The horse plodded past, tugging a rumbling cart weighed down with sixteen-foot rails. I teetered on the embankment. Sensing the swaying weight of the pails pulling me backward, I turned and ran down the few feet of slope, jostling the pails enough that liquid squirted beneath the lids to darken the sides. The heads turned in my direction seemed more concerned for the horse than the tea, though, and since the single-minded creature was well on his way, I adjusted the pole across my shoulder and continued.

There they were, the odd little men working as tirelessly as ants, and equally devoid of enthusiasm. Their movements were small and efficient: shovel bits of rock into a wheelbarrow, move it down the track, dump it between the ties or beside the rails, then return for more. Back and forth, back and forth. No one spoke, for this monotonous routine needed no direction. Another overseer, a potbellied sort in a partially buttoned vest, stood talking with a fellow leader. They were both white. Neither saw me. Since I didn't know what to do with the tea buckets, I lowered them to the ground.

One of the Chinamen noticed and left his wheelbarrow. His wide-brimmed hat hid his face as he approached, and even when he got close and knelt beside the bucket I didn't get much of a look at him. From his padded jacket he took a cup, lifted the bucket's lid, and dipped out some steaming tea. I could see that it didn't have much color to it. Maybe their constitutions were too weak for the stronger stuff.

Moving as silently as a cat, he took himself a little apart, squatted on his heels, and brought the cup to his mouth. Then another worker left his wheelbarrow to come get tea. He, too, sat on his heels sipping. Snippets of muted caterwauling passed between them, though their downcast eyes remained fixed on their teacups. Just as the first worker rose to return to his wheelbarrow, another set down his shovel and came over. Like the first two, he dipped into the tea, sat and chatted, then returned to his work. In this way, in dribs and drabs, the Celestials took their tea in the approaching dusk, but the work of ballasting the tracks never ceased.

Brina had exhausted her nose by then and was flopped next to a stump. She rested her head on her paws, watching me. If it was some sort of appraisal, surely she was disappointed. We'd come all this way to stand guard over tea?

A clopping and rumbling sounded at track height, and I saw the horse named Blind Thomas pass by again. His wagon, now empty, rattled loudly on the rails. I'd never seen a horse work by himself before, but there he was, pulling his supply wagon back and forth with no encouragement from whip or driver.

The liquid was going fast—there were hundreds of the flat-faced workers—when one walked right past the buckets and up to me.

"You bring letter?"

I saw the yellow scarf under his collar and recognized him as the prankster. Was he trying to fun me now? I shook my head.

"Letter for Chun Kwok Keung?"

He didn't sound any more dangerous than a duck, but I kept my guard up and shook my head again.

"For me. From Kwangtung." The way he gulped the tail of each word made his childish English even harder to understand. "You look," he ordered, patting his coat pockets and indicating that I should search mine.

This was foolishness. He was stepping over the line.

"I don't have any letters." And I showed him a fist, which made Brina climb to her feet. "Now, git back to your work."

Stubbornly, he held his place, and I didn't know what to do. I looked past him toward the activity. Surely someone was going to come over to help, but the overseer and his friend were still deep in conversation. I scanned further. Weathered blue jackets swarmed the rails. The foreigners had us outnumbered.

We tossed it around a bit until one of the overseers, the potbellied one, caught sight of the situation and left his conversation to stalk over. Seeing him do that, a Chinaman I'd not noticed before, one dressed in regular pants as well as a black coat, hurried to arrive first. He seemed to have some authority over his mate and sharply quacked some orders that sent Ducks scampering back to work. Then the white overseer arrived. "What's going on here?"

"That was Chun Kwok Keung," said the Chinaman in charge. "He is still looking for his letter."

"Oh, yes." He shook his head. "Shame about that. But the big snows will be here before long; tell him the mail won't be coming up the hill till spring at least." Suddenly turning his attention to me, and with his eyes narrowed, he said, "The railroad's not paying you to eavesdrop, boy. If the tea buckets are empty, take them back and help their cook begin boiling rice." He gave me the once-over as I bent to retrieve the pole and buckets, and I heard him mutter to his Chinaman friend, "Shoulders like that and he only wants to carry tea? They're a lazy bunch, I tell you."

"That is why Ireland does not have a Great Wall."

Both men laughed, and my back stiffened. Brina kept her distance as we returned along the tracks. She had her head down, ashamed. I stomped along, toting up the indignities of the day with each step and wanting to punch something.

Seven

By the time I returned to the Chinese cook I could have boiled water just by looking at it. I was that angry. Lazy bunch, hah! Give me a shovel instead of a pole with buckets and I'd show them—I'd show all of them! Didn't help any that I was sent back into Cisco to fetch another sack of rice. My jaw gritted, my fists flexed. So when I was standing in line at the store and an elbow struck the back of my head, my temper flared instantly. I spun, fists at the ready.

A beefy man in the midst of smoothing his hair and replacing his cap paused. "Easy there, young pup. 'Twasn't a challenge."

I felt the eyes of others and sensed encouragement from some. A fistfight was as much about entertainment as honor. But the man with the cap cocked his head and smiled in such a way that I lowered my fists.

It was the smart thing to do. As frustrated as I was by the day's events, as much as I itched to pound my knuckles into flesh, there were times to fight and times to wait for the fight. It wasn't the same as backing down, because I didn't do that, hadn't for years. I'd won more fights than I'd lost, and even those that I'd lost had left me no more bloodied and bruised than my opponents, no matter their size.

Reliance on my own two fists was something I'd learned from my father back when I was ten. It was before he went away to the war, when he still worked at the brewery. On one cloudy fall day, I remember, I'd been sent by my mother to carry a message to him about the new baby—Ellen her name was—needing more medicine. Thinking about that day always clenched my jaw.

I'd been walking down the alley, poking the toe of my boot through the sodden debris that flooded the passage, when I'd realized a group of older boys was coming toward me. A prickle skipped along my nape, and the black cat that bolted past me toward daylight only reinforced the suspicion that this was a pack of mongrels bent on attack. A bit of me, the part that was instinctive, urged me to join the fleeing cat. But the rest of me rallied my senses, tightened my stomach, and set me on the balls of my feet. To my surprise they sauntered right by, though one boy roughly shoved my shoulder. I kept on walking, though a little faster, in hope of an unnoticed escape.

But I knew they'd halted. "Did you see that?" I heard one growl. "The little Mick shoved me." And in an echoing clatter of boot-shod feet they had me surrounded. Taunts and pokes rained on me from every side. Blindside punches began spinning me around. I swung at each and every one of them.

"Malachy!" An angry voice boomed along the dusky alley, and they all froze to watch my father, bowlegged as a seaman, approach. I could almost envision hackles rising on my father's neck. "Malachy!" he called again.

The one who'd first shoved me grinned sheepishly as he took a cautious step backward. "This your boy, Hugh?"

My father ignored the question. He walked right up to me and clamped a hand on my shoulder, gave each of the boys a lightning-eyed stare, and marched me back down the alley.

"Sorry, Hugh. If we'd known . . ."

Like a policeman with a criminal, my father had marched me the length of the alley, then turned me through a wide entry and into the dark interior of the brewery. The place smelled like soured candy. Still guiding me left and right, nodding perfunctorily to those curious faces we passed, my father took me all the way to the back of the brewery, way back behind the barrels. That's where I received my punishment.

"Jesus, Mary, and Joseph," my father spat, "don't ye ever let me catch ye throwing pansy punches like that, especially when ye're outnumbered. You want to get yourself kilt? Now, listen up, 'cause I'm only going to say this once." He bent his knees and spread his hands, palms open, almost welcoming. "What ye have to do, see, is wait, like this, and watch. Always keeping yeerself at the ready. Always looking to deliver that one punch that decides everything."

And with no warning whatsoever, and with a fist as quick as lightning, my father knocked me flat.

From what I could remember, I'd actually lifted into the air some before slamming onto the floor. My vision exploded, all yellow and white like bits of egg; I tasted the warm salt of my own blood. And in that chilling instant, writhing on my back and gasping, I knew I'd been branded with a lesson that I'd carry with me the rest of my life: I was on my own. It was up to me and me alone to regain my feet and punch the world back. In that momentary blackness words scratched through my mind like lessons on a slate board: Always be watching. Always be waiting. 'Cause you only got one knockout punch.

Eight

The tea delivery didn't last but a day. Seems they wanted one of their own to perform the service, so the next morning a solemn-faced Chinaman hoisted the pole across his bony shoulder and trudged along the rails toward his mates. I was moved farther up the line and added to a clean-up crew, which was only a girl's job, no two ways about it.

The hard work had been done here, trees and rocks already blasted to bits. Now I and a dozen other men, and not the stoutest sort, mind you—there were a lot of graybeards bending their backs beside me—gathered splintered limbs and upturned stones, dragged out stumps, and raked away clods. We swept those slopes clean for a hundred feet on either side of where the rails would be laid. I know that because Mr. Jessop, our boss, measured the span daily, and if his tape passed over even the promise of an upstart sapling, we were sent back with our shovels.

During my first days of railroading, the weather remained mostly sunny though bracingly brisk. It stayed cold enough, in fact, to protect what drifts of snow peeked from the shade of heavy pine boughs. Then, in the space of one afternoon, a miserable storm blew in and settled. It pelted us with stinging sleet and painted a slushy mix of ice and snow atop newly muddied ground. But the rail work didn't stop. We trudged and slid and did our best with numb fingers to keep tugging away the frozen remains of the forest. The storm was just as stubborn and didn't let up either.

A lot of the men disappeared then. I'd heard them complaining about the working conditions and the pay, and I admit to listening with keen ears to their talk of gold just beyond the next mountain. Bending your back there earned you heaps more than an ache, they grumbled. I suspected George and his friend had already made the leap, because I hadn't seen them since that day the train let us off in Cisco. Maybe they'd just signed on for the free ride up the mountain. Others had. I wondered at times if they were in their own camp somewhere, sitting atop bags of gold nuggets, or if they were back in town again, cozied up to a stove and hugging hot cups of sugared coffee. But when the rain's hammering your head and the snot's running out of your nose, those kinds of thoughts only make you colder, so I set them aside.

New faces appeared, though, and among them was Patrick Joyce, a fellow Irishman. He climbed into our sleeping car early one evening and, eyeing the stacked bunks that reeked of musty clothes and midnight farts, asked in stone-faced humor, "Is it funnin' me ye are? I was promised me own feather bed."

"Oh, that would be the top bunk over in the corner," one of the others replied, jerking his thumb in that direction and provoking a round of laughter.

Patrick heaved his pack up onto it, retrieved a deck of cards, and shuffling them absently, strolled over to take a seat among us. He was as thin as a lamppost (though I was soon to discover he was as strong as an ox) and wore an easy smile and ill-fitting clothes: fraying sleeves that stopped short of his wrists and a belt that had to be knotted twice. His gray eyes, heavily lashed, didn't miss a thing. I was also to learn that he pocketed his observations for later use.

The very next day brought a few more arrivals, and one was Jesse Stephens, a cowboy who, during the introductions, claimed to have ridden all over the country, from St. Louis, Missouri, through most of Texas, and on up to Montana. When he joined our group and stretched his legs out, his pants rode up to reveal colorfully dyed, tall-heeled dress boots featuring the stitched design of a rope lassoing stars.

"I'm blinded!" someone howled, keeling over in a dramatic charade. Another inquired, "Were they all out of the brown ones?"

Jesse's round face, heavily creased from his saddle days squinting into the sun, I supposed, split into a grin. He spat a stream of tobacco juice across the room and said, "I take it you gentlemen aren't familiar with the clothing preferences of cattle barons. See, I'm just wintering here for the pay. Already got a spread up in Wyoming; prettiest, greenest land you ever laid eyes on. And I already own two of the fastest mares this side of Texas. Going to start me a cattle ranch as soon as I build up my stake." He removed a deck of cards from his coat pocket and scanned the room. "Any of you fellers gambling men?"

From the other side of the circle, Patrick looked up and grinned.

The railroad's sleeping cars provided shelter from winter's onslaught, though not much warmth. Each day, we climbed down the metal steps in the still-dark morning and headed straight for the camp's cook to huddle over a breakfast of fried meat and potatoes. Patrick continued to moan that he'd been hoodwinked ("I was promised eggs and tomatoes! Where are my tomatoes?")

while Jesse lowered his head over his plate and scooped food into his mouth faster than he could possibly swallow it. It was a daily wonder that he didn't choke.

For some reason—and I suppose it was my curiosity again—I'd gotten into the habit of glancing up the rails first thing. No matter the hour, the white tents that the Celestials used for sleeping—they preferred them to railcars, I was told—were a canvas for the comings and goings of these curious people. A campfire always crackled and shadowy figures moved past it or hunched around it. Sometimes, if the wind was right, you caught a whiff of greens being cooked and other velvety aromas not easily described, and after the tenth day straight of you pushing fried meat and potatoes down your throat your stomach sort of begged you to take a stroll toward those inviting smells.

Brina didn't mind the breakfast monotony. She crawled from under the sleeping car each morning, as soon as the first one of us stepped out, and she was always wagging her tail so hard it shook her whole body. She wriggled like she had no spine, in fact, like she was a fish striving upstream. The men took to her. They patted her head, and Patrick especially always said "Good morning to ye, Brina" before stumbling through the dark toward his coffee. I hung back and watched her search one face after another, because I knew she was waiting for me, and that filled my chest.

"Hey, lass," I'd say finally while she embarrassed herself by banging against my knees and almost toppling me over. "There's a good girl now." And we'd parade up to the breakfast line together.

"Get that no-account cur away from me food or I'll be serving her up to ye on a plate," the cook, Swifty O'Shea, always grumbled. That was the best he could do for a greeting. He'd wave his big iron spoon at Brina, who only took herself over to the kindling pile to sit and grin, her tongue hanging out and dripping, because she knew the game. Swifty kept looking over his shoulder at her and shaking his spoon, but she neither shied nor begged. She didn't have to. As soon as the last man had eaten his breakfast and turned in his plate and headed off to work, Swifty prepared two more plates. One he piled high with potatoes drowned in vinegar, and the other with the burnt scrapings from the skillet and the fatty bits of leftover meat. Then he and Brina sat down to their own quiet breakfast. I know this for a fact, because when Brina stopped following me out to work after the first couple of days, I sauntered back to look for her, and that's how I found the two of them: seated side by side, savoring their meal and each other's company.

God love a dog.

Nine

Hiking out each morning through a forest of spires that pointed toward the heavens made you feel puny, I had to admit, like you were in the presence of God.

But bringing them down made you feel better. It made you feel like you *were* God when you brought one of those giants crashing to earth. And the railroad gave us an arsenal of weapons for accomplishing the feat: axes and saws and, most powerful of all, blasting powder.

After a week or so on the job, I'd been pulled from my clean-up crew to join the men and Celestials working well ahead of the tie laying, the ones doing the difficult work of felling trees, blasting stumps, and leveling a grade for the future rails. And I'd gotten my first pay: nine dollars and twenty-five cents in gold coins. I was ashamed to admit, of course, that I'd lost nearly half of it in the poker game Patrick and Jesse had organized on Saturday night.

I knew I was supposed to be sending my money home to Ma and the others, but I wasn't feeling too bad about it, because Pa had always been the gambling sort. "A penny *played* is a penny *turned*—to *profit!*"—he'd liked to quip. And well I remember him spreading his winnings on the kitchen table after a night out and Ma throwing her arms around his neck and kissing his cheek. It was Jesse who had gathered most of the coins for himself this past Saturday, but I knew I'd have a chance to win back my pay in another couple of weeks, so I wasn't bothered.

As we tromped toward our worksite on this particular morning, the scent of resin, the spilled blood of our slaughtered foes, hung heavy and thick in the gloom. Even though it was still early, a multitude of axes were already biting into soft pine in the distance. There was a rhythm to their hunger: *thud, thud, thud.* It was as steady as a heartbeat. And that heartbeat reverberated through the forest—*thud, thud, thud*—until there came a wrenching gasp and the axes fell silent. An awful screech preceded a lengthy ripping sound that split the morning. Branches clawed and crashed through the canopy with tremendous noise. Then—*boom!*—the ground beneath me shifted with the tree's impact and the vibrations raced through the soles of my boots.

A brief silence. Men voiced their satisfaction. Then the hungry axes resumed their rhythm.

Patrick and Jesse worked on one of the felling crews; I and some other men I was getting to know made up a crew that blasted stumps out of the ground and, Mother of God, that was something! At the first explosion that I'd experienced, the skin on my neck had prickled so tightly my hair stood on end. Singed air had scorched my throat, and an unexpected storm of splintered bark, dislodged rocks, and tangled rootwads had battered the hat on my head. I'd run for cover like a frightened rabbit. And I wasn't the only one.

But that was then and this was now and, splitting off from Patrick and Jesse, I made my way toward the stump-clearing site with ample confidence. The day's work was soon sorted out for us, and the first series of blasts went well, with one of the Celestials routinely lighting the fuse, then dashing to safety while the cord's tail sparked and hissed like the devil's very own. I'd been told that the Chinese people had a long history with black powder and that's why they were tapped for this dangerous work: They did seem to be good at it. So, time after time that morning, stubborn tree stumps shot into the air to explode into a black shower of shredded fragments.

Until right before noon. As usual, our crew was crouched behind standing trees and other stumps, peering out from beneath angled elbows and splayed fingers. Waiting. I heard my own quickened breathing in the frozen interlude and watched puffs of vapor curl round us like smoke. I was gauging the seconds until the explosion—we all were—and then, when those seconds stretched too long, tensing with the knowledge that we had a situation. Eyes began shifting sideways, questioning.

"What's happened?" I murmured to Nicholas Boyle, who was crouched beside me.

He blew warm air into his cupped hands and shook his head. "The damp must have snuffed the spark."

Across the slope, heads began poking into the air like those of gophers.

"So what do we do?" I asked.

"*We* don't have to do anything, thank God," Nicholas said. He nodded toward the stand of trees shielding the Celestial portion of our crew. "That's why the railroad hired *them*."

With a sickening sense of dread I realized that one of the Chinamen was, at that very moment, being tapped to approach the unexploded powder and investigate. And the unlucky soul who rose happened to be that Ducks character, looking surprisingly calm given the life-threatening task assigned to him. I admit I both admired his bravery and feared for his safety.

He eyed the slope. Then, like a cat, he began creeping silently, warily, his body hunched in anticipation.

Nicholas, rubbing his shoulder like it had a sudden pain, moaned. "Oh, Lord, I'm getting a bad feeling."

"What do you mean?"

"It's the gift of me grandmam." He left off the rubbing to lace his fingers across his hat and to rock back and forth. His forehead wrinkled like he was trying to do sums in his head. "I get a sense for when something bad is going to happen."

"You do?"

"Yes, I do. Are you doubting me?"

I shook my head.

"Because I can prove it. You've seen Mr. Strobridge and his eye patch, right?"

Oh, that I had.

"Well, I was there the day he lost his eye, and I knew it was going to happen before it happened, I swear. My shoulder was just as twitchy and sore then as it is now." He paused to see if I believed him, and I gave an encouraging nod. "We were working Bloomer Cut, that narrow pass after the big trestle at Newcastle."

I remembered. The deep, chiseled pass was so narrow, you could just about touch the rock walls from your seat on the train.

"Hell of a project, that. Barrel after barrel of black powder we threw at the rock, but it might as well have been black pepper for all the progress we were making.

Took months to cut the whole pass, and it was only about eight hundred yards. Anyway," he said, slapping at his head like he was trying to get water out of his ears, "on this one day when my shoulder was warning me of something bad on the horizon, we'd just lit another fuse and there were three of us waiting for it to go off. But nothing happened. Just like now."

Both of us paused to watch Ducks working his way cautiously up the mountainside. Clods of damp soil gave way beneath his feet. My heart skipped a beat or two.

"Mr. Strobridge was on-site that day," Nicholas continued, "overseeing the blasting, and he came down hard on our foreman, Denis. 'What did you do wrong?' he starts bellowing when the powder didn't light. 'Nothing,' says Denis. 'Then go fix it,' says Mr. Strobridge.

"Of course Denis was scared—and he shouldn't have been the one sent—but he takes a couple of steps in the direction of the burned fuse and then stops. He knows he's gonna get himself killed if that powder goes off unexpected. Well, Mr. Strobridge, he starts spitting and cursing like the dickens and says some things I wouldn't repeat in confession, and he goes stomping right by the man. Course Jerry O'Malley, who was always bragging about his great feats in the war, decides to go too. Not me, no sirree. I sat where I was 'cause I knew what was going to happen. And it did."

His eyes got wide like he was relating the sighting of a ghost. "The three of 'em had just gotten to the rock, and Denis was poking at the drill hole with his crowbar, when all of a sudden there's a loud shot—*crack!*—like a gun fired right next to your ear. The quavering ground almost shook me outta my boots, and the sky started raining rocks and dirt and spitting grit everywhere.

"I gave it no mind, of course, and ran out to help. And, och, what I saw! There's Denis blown back flat on the ground and missing half his face, and young Jerry O'Malley, with his shirt ripped to rags, swaying on his knees. And there's Mr. Strobridge standing and holding one hand over his eye, blood coming through his fingers and trickling down his cheek and his neck. And you know what he does?"

I couldn't begin to imagine.

"He just blinks at me a couple of times like he's surprised. And then he digs his fingers into the bloody eye socket and claws out a chunk of granite. Stuffs the socket with his handkerchief and hollers, 'Move your lazy arse, Boyle, and get some assistance for these men!'"

I worked my mouth but nothing came out. Jesus, Mary, and Joseph! What did you say to such a story? When I got my tongue moving at last, I asked, "What happened to your friends?"

Nicholas gazed into the distance. "Denis was dead

where he fell," he related solemnly. "We put his body on the supply train back to Sacramento that same afternoon. Jerry O'Malley broke his jaw and lost some teeth. Ate nothing but porridge for a month or more. I don't know where he is now." His blue eyes fell on me. "I'm telling you, Malachy, if you're not mindful of the dangers of this work, of doing battle with this land, it'll chew you up and spit you out without a look back."

As if to hush us, Ducks peered over his shoulder and frowned. He seemed to heave a little sigh then, gather his courage, and continue his upward crawl. Nicholas gave an allover shiver like a wet dog and closed his eyes, waiting for his prophesied catastrophe.

It didn't happen. Not that morning, at least. Ducks got the fuse going again and managed to escape the almost immediate blast with an acrobatic tumble down the slope. We descended on the remains of that stump with axes and shovels, and continued clearing the mountainside. The California sky turned a brilliant blue.

Just before the noon break was called, our boss, Mr. Haines, came by to look over our progress. A gruff man by nature, he nodded approvingly and took some notes in a little book he carried. He spoke to one of the senior members of the crew, a bear of a man with shaggy black hair that poked from his collar and cuffs, and together they examined the supplies available for the afternoon's work. I was heaving all my weight against a stubborn root when Mr. Haines hollered.

"You there, Mr. Gormley!"

I hurried over. "Yes, sir?"

"Mr. Burroughs here says you're doing a fine job, and I've witnessed the same, so we're rewarding you with a break." He pointed to two axes lying on the ground, both showing dulled blades. "Carry those back to the supply car, if you will, and have Mr. Finnell sharpen them. If he can't do it at once, then tell him to provide you with two new axes, understood?"

I nodded and, swelling with pride, hefted the axes over one shoulder as I'd seen the more experienced lumbermen do. Setting off, I thought how good it felt to be called out by name, to be recognized. It felt good, too, to stretch my back and legs; a welcome change from the grueling work of wrestling tree stumps.

Chopping and sawing was going on all around me, and I didn't notice the great ripping sound overhead until a figure in blue pajamas came hurtling toward me. In the next instant the air left my lungs as I was knocked to the ground. My chin hit snow and frozen dirt, and man alive, that stung! Needled branches lashed my legs while shredded bark pelted my head, my arms, my trousered legs—all of me that wasn't covered by the Chinaman. As the stranger clung to my back, his long pigtail slipped across my cheek. His garlicky breath warmed my neck. "It is okay, *di-di*. Little brother."

Protest surged through me. "Give over!" I grunted, and gave him the elbow, though he was rolling off already. He jumped to his feet.

Ducks. Again. Was he to be the hero of *every* hour?

"I need check pocket for letter," he joked, grinning.

I wasn't in the mood. Though we were probably two of the youngest members of the crew, he obviously thought of himself as older and my protector. Well, I wasn't having it, especially from the likes of him; so when he offered his small hand, I ignored it and climbed to my feet unassisted.

"You no break bone?" he asked with what sounded like genuine concern. Touching various points on his own body, he prompted, "You no hurt here . . . or here?"

Before I could answer, the felling crew came clambering through the needled boughs of the fallen pine.

"Are you two okay?"

"Land sakes, you escaped by no more than a whisker!"

"McConley," their boss hollered down the length of the tree, "I told you to mind your back cuts! Now you've nearly killed a man. Do you see that? And the blasted tree's gone the wrong way."

Ducks's smile slowly faded as he was jostled to the

side. I saw him take a step backward, go tumbling over a web of springy boughs, and barely manage to keep his balance.

Patrick was shoving his way forward, Jesse in his wake, when someone in the group hollered, "Aye, and weren't they spooning like a pair of lovebirds?"

That brought a grin to Patrick's face. "The two of you will be setting up house, I reckon," he added with a wink.

Not to be left out, Jesse quipped, "Will you start wearing the blue pajama pants now?"

I felt my face flush hot. The blathering idiots.

"All right," the boss shouted. "Back to your work, every last one of you. And I mean this instant, or I'm assigning you to the dump carts!"

The men scattered at once. Plucking my hat from the ground and slapping away the mud, I fitted it onto my head. The soaked band did nothing to cool my injured pride. I retrieved the axes and began tramping away toward the supply car, taking just one curious glance over my shoulder to see Ducks marching stiffly in the opposite direction.

Ten

The mountains didn't give up their battle. If they couldn't knock us back with trees or chase us off with cold, they could bury us under snow. And they did. Storm upon storm slammed our camp, piling the snow ever higher. Rushing winds spun it into drifts that swallowed trains whole.

"Never seen the likes of it," said the local men, greasing their wind-reddened faces and rubbing the frost from their beards. "It's one for the ages."

This new battle called for new weapons, so we set down our axes and our saws and took up shovels. From sunup to sundown we struggled through the chest-deep stuff, trying to clear the tracks. The scene was a stark one: men in black coats working tirelessly against a blinding white landscape, putting up a fight just to get the supply cars through.

But it was a losing effort. The moment we scooped up the snow and heaved it out of the way, the wind flung it right back into our faces, sifted it inside our collars, piled it around our feet. Day after blasted day we shoveled, but each morning we arose to find all our work was undone. The tracks were nowhere to be seen, and in some places the drifts rose as high as three men. Beginning to weary, we took up our shovels and started over.

On sunny days the snow dazzled with the brilliance of a thousand mirrors, and for a brief time, I think, we felt lifted up by its beauty. But you couldn't blink away that glare, and after a few hours the sun's rays narrowed into a stabbing pain, like icicles to the eyes. We were blinded. And I mean *blinded*.

I'd never welcomed nightfall as much as I did then. My eyes were so swollen most evenings that I had to tip my head to see if my fork was hitting my dinner plate. By the time I stumbled into my bunk, my eyes burned like they were on fire, like someone had packed them with powder and struck a match. In the darkness, fiery dragonflies zigged and zagged, drawing red streaks across my closed lids.

The darkness of the sleeping car was a heavenly haven after all that white, and most of us fell to snoring right away. But not me. Ever since that tree nearly crushed me, I'd become acutely aware of what could

happen. I heard the mountains creaking and groaning all night long beneath their blanket of snow. Restless. Planning a different sort of attack on our small camp. And those sounds kept me fidgeting for hours. Did no one else sense the danger?

Then, very early in the blackness of one morning, the mountains sought their revenge. A distant rumble, disguised at first as thunder and meant to fool us, stealthily built into a full-blown charge. An enormous whoosh preceded a bruising thud that sent our sleeping car rocking.

"What the—?"

"Get up! Get up! Everybody up!"

Out into the dark we scrambled, pulling on coats and yanking on unlaced boots. There stood Brina, braced and at the ready. "C'mon, lass!" I said, and we hurried down the tracks with the others.

The starlit sky shone upon a massive white drift of snow curtaining the car right behind ours as well as most of the car beyond. The men inside were trapped. Instinctively, we plunged into the frozen ocean, waving shovels instead of oars.

"Hello, there! We're coming!" shouted a fellow named Ethan, taking charge. He floundered the length of the drift, calling and listening, then turned to me. "Start digging here!"

I fought my way forward. Although the snow was as wet and heavy as cement, I scooped with a fury, all the while thinking, *Good Lord, these men have been buried alive!* Would we reach them in time? Patrick and Jesse joined in as Ethan beckoned more men to the next car. Catching wind of our frenzy, even Brina energetically clawed the snow for a time.

It didn't matter that we didn't come upon the door. When the first shovel connected with the car, we tapped along the frame until we found glass, and smashed right through it. The trapped men were only too happy to squeeze through the window, tumble into the snow, and escape their short-term coffin.

After that, no one slept. The cook fired the stove, and we ate beans and beef in exhausted silence, knowing we would finish the day as we'd already begun it: shoveling. Jesse got out his cards and shuffled them lackadaisically. I knew he was hoping for a game, and part of me wanted to get back the money I'd lost. That was what my pa would have urged me to do. But in my mind I was recalling those mornings that he'd spread his winnings across the table, and I was seeing beyond Ma's hugs and watching her hungrily try to scrape a few of those precious coins into her apron. There'd never been enough money in our home, but there had been plenty of hunger, so I was thinking that maybe it'd be better to collect some

more pay and get my pockets full before gambling any more of it.

I got to thinking, too, about how nice it would be to stroll through the door and spread a fistful of my gold coins across the table, hear the squeals of Ellen and Margaret and Ma, and maybe even Sean, if he wasn't too grown up by then to squeal. It'd be nice, then, to sit around the stove and listen to Ma tell her stories of growing up on a sheep farm in Ireland, how she gave names to all the lambs and they followed her around, switching their little tails and calling to her like she was their own mother.

From across the room Jesse caught my eye and raised a questioning brow. He fanned the cards. I shook my head. No, my next pay was going straight to New York as soon as I could get to a town and send it.

But that snow slide led to ever more anxious nights for me. Why was the company even keeping us here? Obviously, our human efforts were too puny; the rails weren't advancing an inch. All we did was shovel snow day after day, only to have it snow again at night. Certainly, with all these storms there'd be more snow slides. That fear wormed so deep inside me that many a night I barely dozed. In my dreams my sleepless legs kicked against an icy froth that I couldn't possibly escape while my fingers sought—but never reached—the safety

of the bunk frame. Tossing and turning, I suffered an ago-
nizing death over and over.

Sometimes the night's cold was an actual relief,
because I'd awaken to find my twisted blanket had fallen
to the floor. After retrieving it, I'd climb back into my
bunk, thank the saints for sparing my life, and try mightily
to prop my eyelids open until dawn. At least then I might
see the snow slide that was coming for me, and run.

Brina shivered too, but not (to my knowledge, anyway) from nightmares. Her tight coat offered such little
warmth that when the wind blew it chilled her to the
marrow. Swifty O'Shea, her favorite cook, had turned in
his apron at the first heavy snow, and his replacement
was a sour sort having nothing to do with dogs. So Brina
followed me everywhere. She got in line when we set
out of a morning, jackrabbiting through our deep tracks
in the snow. While we shoveled, she'd nose out a sunny
spot if she could, spin four or five times, patting down a
snow nest, then curl up. I could see her trembling as one
squinting eye marked my every move. But sometimes,
if the snow was blowing, I couldn't see her at all, she'd
be so frosted in white. That was some kind of faithful, I
tell you, and I wasn't sure I was deserving. But when the
men nodded approval—*she's a grand dog, she is*—I did
fill with pride.

Come dusk, I always sat on the metal steps of the

sleeping car and dug pea-size balls of packed snow from her paws. She offered up each one just like a lady extending her hand, then gently licked mine in gratitude. A cloud of vapor escaped her mouth, and my chapped skin glistened just as brightly as her pink tongue.

One evening, after we'd hiked farther up the tracks to clear an area for a shed—a small number of horses were going to be stabled in the mountains through the winter for work in the tunnels—and tramped home in the cold blue twilight, I found two of Brina's paws bleeding. The few men left in our sleeping car—those who hadn't set down their shovels during the miseries of the past weeks and fled back to Cisco—invited her inside. Ever the lady, she wagged her appreciation and padded to a private corner.

But the snows continued with such persistence that the railroad work stalled. The mountain had us on our backs for sure. More and more, the talk at meals returned to the enormous folly of this venture. Even if the tracks eventually did get built, men muttered, blizzards would bury them each and every winter. And the way the stuff came down in tons, heavier even than cement, a half-dozen locomotives couldn't ram through it. Was this entire coast-to-coast railroad going to be a summer lark only?

It looked that way, because word came up the rails

finally that almost all the work was being suspended until the spring thaw. The mountains had won. We were retreating.

Smiles creased windburned faces. To a man, we were thoroughly bone weary, fed up with the cold and the monotony, and tired of losing.

"I'll be in Roseville for Christmas," sighed Ethan, packing his haversack. "I'll see my newborn son. You, Daniel?"

"San Francisco," he answered with a grin. "No snow! Had enough servings of this stuff for two lifetimes."

"What about you, Jesse? Staying or going?"

"Oh, I reckon I'll winter here. It's no worse than Wyoming. Been doin' some figurin', and I'm gonna need to add to my stake to put up some proper fencing. Can't have my nice mares running off with a band of no-account mustangs."

"Guess I'll stay put, too," Patrick said. "See if I can win back some of my poker money before Jesse goes riding off to Wyoming with it." He turned to me. "You?"

I shrugged. Hearing Ethan and Daniel talk about going home for Christmas had me feeling low. It was kind of a childish feeling, because building a railroad through the wilderness is what I'd signed on for, and such work didn't usually come with holiday trips home, so I didn't want to admit to my longings. Patrick guessed, though. In a gentle manner he said, "New York's too far away, isn't it?"

I nodded glumly and reached down to adjust my bootlaces, fiddling with them until the heat left my eyes.

Soon afterward, the railroad extended a bottom-of-the-barrel offer, and Brina and I, along with a few other frostbitten souls, exchanged a vista of blinding white snow for a home in a sightless black tunnel.

Eleven

"Tangyuan?"

The words broke the uncomfortable silence within the candlelit tunnel.

"*Tangyuan?* Rice-ball soup?" One of the Chinamen was extending a small ceramic bowl in my direction, and my stomach gurgled acceptance—loud enough, I think, for the huddled workers to hear—before my head could nod. It was that quiet.

Elsewhere inside the mountain's guts, hammers and picks pinged with the regularity of a pendulum clock. But in my tunnel the work had halted for some sort of ritual. It was temporary, I hoped, or Mr. Sikes would have our hides. Normally the Celestials and I took pains not to look directly at one another, let alone speak, though we practically bumped shoulders in our comings and goings. So this invitation was special, and

I left the horse and cart I was in charge of to saunter over and accept it. Brina rose and pranced at my side, because now that even the sour-tempered cook had returned to civilization, she had to depend on me for her well-being. That was harsh punishment indeed, for I was not skilled with the frying pan.

The Chinamen had always been frightened of her, I think, especially in the close quarters of the tunnel. With suspicious eyes they watched her approach and like birds hunched in a flock, they reacted warily as one: shoulders moved to shield their bowls, knees lifted to protect their laps.

There were twelve of them, eight squatting in a semicircle on the rock floor, and four more sitting on scaffolding above, their legs dangling. I got the impression there might have been a discussion about me—and some disagreement—because the lipless mouths were clamped in a united grimace. You couldn't be certain, though, since they wore solemn expressions as a matter of habit. Some heads were turned away, having no part in the decision. But I accepted the offered treat and nodded, my stomach gurgling its gratitude.

"*Dongzhi.* Day and night same now," the man said in a singsong voice. He added gestures, apparently meant to clarify his gibberish. "Yin and yang," he said, weighing his hands in the air. "Soon yang grow more strong, day come more long." A glint of excitement pulled on his features.

I had no idea who Yin and Yang were, but the Chinamen were all watching me. Even those who'd turned away peeked over their shoulders.

"Eat soup, honor ancestors," another said, motioning for me to begin.

There was a round doughy something floating in the bowl's broth, but no spoon. What was I supposed to do? I glanced over the rim. They all had their bowls at chin level and at the ready, no spoons in sight, so I followed along and lifted the bowl to my lips. Apologizing silently to my ma, I slurped a taste of the broth, which turned out to be some sort of molasses in hot water and not bad at all. I slurped some more, which seemed to give them the okay to begin, then spun the bowl sharply and managed to snatch up the doughy ball with my teeth as it floated past. It, too, was sweet as well as chewy.

I nodded my approval to the little men on the ground and then those up on the scaffolding. One of them was Ducks. We hadn't spoken to each other since discovering that we'd been assigned to work this same shift in this same tunnel. He was watching me now with the impassive face of his countrymen, sipping from his

bowl with one hand while casually swinging a sledgehammer between his legs with the other. I'd come to
realize that I owed him a rather big thank-you, but I was
having trouble stepping forward.

Boots came tramping through the darkness. "I don't
like what I'm not hearing!" It was our boss, Mr. Sikes.
"There'd better be a man stretched out cold to warrant
a work stoppage or I'm fining the whole lot of you."

The Chinamen scrambled. I scrambled. My new
work was moving rubble out of the tunnel with a horse
and a dump cart, and I already had them backed into
place and awaiting the next load. The horse, by another
coincidence, was Blind Thomas, the one who'd nearly
run me over when I'd first started. I guess the railroad's
reasoning was that, since he couldn't see anyway, he
wouldn't mind working in a tunnel all through the dark
winter. But he had his opinions, I'm telling you, and now
flicked his ears at the shouted threats. He straightened
his hip but pursed his lips in annoyance.

Mr. Sikes came into view, waving his arms at all of
us. "What's the holdup? Get back to work!" I made a
show of repositioning Blind Thomas, and the horse obe-
diently nudged the cart a little closer to the tunneling
work, though his ears were pinned flat against his head.
Sugar went farther with him than vinegar.

"Where's Chang?" Mr. Sikes demanded of me.

That was the Chinamen's boss, who could speak both English and Chinese and so communicate with both them and us.

"Went to see about supplies."

The squat man fumed. "I'll be having a few words with him, too, I will." His cheek bulged with the wad of tobacco he had stashed there, and his thick brown beard waggled. He stalked toward the deepest part of the tunnel, examining the progress with narrowed eyes. "I'm docking all your pay," he said over his shoulder, "which isn't arriving until Monday. And I'm docking yours, too, Gormley."

"But—"

"Not a word from you. You're white—you should see that they keep to their work." Returning to the base of the scaffold, he brandished a fist at the men now busily hammering away up there. "I know you yellow monkeys can't understand a word I'm saying, but you'll understand this." And he grabbed hold of the structure and shook it hard. The man was as strong as a bear, and the scaffolding rocked so violently that the four Chinamen had to hug the rock wall for fear of falling. Tiny shards of granite shimmied to the edge of the platform and plunked to the tunnel floor. Dust clouded the air. "Now, work!" he roared, and turned to leave.

No more than a pair of heartbeats passed when

a sledgehammer, iron head first, slammed into the very spot where Mr. Sikes had been standing.

It could have been an accident, and everyone paused to look upward, including me. There stood Ducks, his palm open and empty, his face still hiding his thoughts.

Twelve

For the rest of that day, tension in the tunnel grew as thick as the dust, choking back conversation. Anger pulsed in the furious clang of sledgehammer on drill, in the monotonous stomp of boots, in the deafening crash of loosened rock. We'd been tasked with chiseling through a solid granite mountain, for land sakes. Such a feat had never been achieved anywhere in the world. Anywhere. If the pace wasn't fast enough for Mr. Sikes, maybe he needed to take up a hammer himself!

Yet the practiced battle between the Chinamen and this mountain, the precisely coordinated effort, was as mesmerizing to watch as any good boxing match. Although it was well into December, those Celestials worked themselves to a glistening sweat and still never paused, not even for their tea. They just stripped off their heavy jackets and cuffed their sleeves and continued beating their bitterness to gravel. I came to admire them.

Ignorant of the dangers he risked, Mr. Sikes returned repeatedly and without warning to shout "Faster!" and "Chop-chop!" When he unfolded his ruler against the rock, twelve pairs of eyes measured the distance to his back. Without fail he hollered something akin to "You've gained but three inches—not good enough!" before scurrying on to another tunnel. The next sledgehammer to hit the drill rang out with particular force.

For our parts, Thomas and Brina and I kept our noses pointed toward the exit and focused on hauling the tunnel's guts outside and spilling them down the mountains' own flanks. We'd adopted a pretty efficient routine of our own, and so the next morning, as soon as the last shovelful of granite rubble had been heaved into the dump cart, I clucked my tongue and said, "Come along, Thomas." The obedient horse leaned into his harness, and the leather squealed. The dump cart groaned, overwhelmed by its heavy load. Thomas lifted one big knee and planted a hoof, then lifted the other, straining against the weight. At this next step his iron shoe lost hold, and for precarious seconds he scrambled like a giant balancing on ice. The racket turned pigtailed heads. "Easy, lad," I said to him. "You can do it." He grunted and with a great effort gathered himself. A few rapid-fire steps and he found purchase again. The gravel that crunched and popped beneath the spoke wheels disintegrated into twin trails of white powder. But humiliation pinned his ears as he resumed his work: He had his own pride.

I slipped my fingers inside the cheek strap of his bridle. Not that he needed the guidance, or the comfort. He was too independent, I'd learned, the sort of animal who liked to think for himself. No matter what work the railroad gave him, Blind Thomas, once he understood it, marched forward as smartly as any horse with two good eyes. A rare creature, he was, and the men admired him. And that made me extra proud to partner with him. No, I slipped my fingers inside the cheek strap that morning because it felt good. The heat trapped in the thick, shaggy jaw hairs warmed my cold fingers, and so we started walking shoulder to shoulder as if we shared a harness.

Blind Thomas, I'd also come to know, was a creature who needed his routine; everything had to be done in the same order every day. He was just like old Mr. Connally, that tortoise of a teacher I'd once had, who every morning had to carefully lay out his chalk and his ruler and his books in a straight row and square them up before clapping his hands and beginning class. The way Thomas was swiveling his ears now, twitching them back and forth like Mr. Connally twitched his black moustache, told me he was annoyed at the hiccup in the morning's routine.

"You're fine," I assured him, and let go of the bridle long enough to stroke his furry neck. Was that the slightest answering pressure against my hand? I wanted to think he appreciated my attentions, but this horse, at least in harness, was all business. And since he'd kept plodding on, I had to quicken my step to catch up. Brina trotted behind.

"Sponge cake and blackberries again last night," I told Thomas, my mouth watering at the memory. "That's what I dreamed of. They were served on a yellow plate."

If someone had told me two months ago I'd be sharing my thoughts with a blind carthorse or a ribby dog, I'd have popped him a good one. But truth was, I was lonesome up here in the tunnel. While conversation had never come easily to me—seemed I always got tongue-tied at the worst possible moments—it was hardly an option now. I was the sole white man working this shift, and the twelve Celestials, especially since the incident with Mr. Sikes, exchanged only necessary conversation, all of it gibberish: a brief squawking or cackle among themselves while they repositioned the drill or shoveled the granite chunks into the cart. It irked me to stand alongside Thomas as uncomprehending as a toddler in diapers. So much for Yin and Yang and shared bowls of soup.

Even Mr. Chang, who could speak English when he chose to do so, passed his narrow eyes right across me upon his visits, dismissing me as some mute attachment to the carthorse, and that ruffled my feathers some. He was an efficient little man who wore spectacles secured by a braided red ribbon that perfectly matched the red silk trim on his long sleeves. He spoke to his countrymen in tumbling syllables that bumped and stretched and whined, delivering his orders or the week's news or possibly his grandmother's recipe for rice dumplings, for all I could understand. His fellow Celestials chattered back. And when they did, something happened: The thin-lipped, solemn masks they wore melted away like snow in the sunshine. An eyebrow lifted. A smile flashed. Suddenly one was noticeably taller, another bowlegged. Having dropped their curtain of secrecy, they stood astonishingly clear as individuals. Ducks was the wag of the group—I could tell by the way his mates laughed at his quips and elbowed his ribs, and by the way Mr. Chang rolled his eyes. Another was the gossip; the men all leaned in when he whispered to them between furtive glances over his shoulder. I was certain they whispered about me, because, in this tunnel at least, I'd become the foreigner. That chafed too.

When Mr. Chang left, the Chinamen returned to hammering away at the drills they positioned by hand,

and to loading chunks of granite from the most recent blast into the dump cart. No words were exchanged with me; eyes never lifted. So it seemed that if I didn't take my tongue out for some exercise, I might forget how to speak at all, and come spring thaw I just might emerge from this tunnel as mute as a mole. That's how Blind Thomas and I came to talking on our trips back and forth. Or I talked and he listened, God bless his silent soul.

"They were juicy berries, Thomas, the biggest you ever saw, and I was just taking a spoon to them when, and this you're not going to believe, I noticed a fuse—a fuse, of all things!—running from the plate to the edge of the table, then down to the floor and out the door. And then I saw this crackling bit of fire coming along it. Course I knew I should run, but I wanted them berries, so—"

Thomas's ears pricked, not at what I was saying but toward what lay ahead. He couldn't *see* the change, of course, but maybe he could smell it. Did snow have a smell? I left off my babbling to raise my nose and sniff but caught little more than a sense of stale cold. And heavy, muffled air. But soon enough the clip-clop of Thomas's hooves became a *scrinch-scrunch* as we entered the half-lit, slightly bluish tube. See, we were leaving the rock tunnel, the one we were drilling into the mountain, for a snow tunnel, the only passage through the towering mounds the winter was regularly delivering. Thomas never hesitated.

It was odd to have snow on all sides of you, even over your head, and we walked in a cottony sort of quiet until I continued with my dream. "So there was this popping sound, and I fell out of my bed—don't ask me how I got there, and don't you smirk, either—and it wasn't the fuse at all, it was a champagne bottle!" The snowy walls enwrapped my words and gobbled them up. "Someone had cracked it open—broke the glass neck right off—and flooded the room. I heard a train whistle, I remember—again, don't ask me—and champagne bubbles went everywhere. I awoke sneezing."

Brina looked up at me and grinned, her pink tongue fluttering, and I gave her a pat on the head. Blind Thomas, still wearing a smirk—at least in my view—trudged on.

Up ahead, a beam of sunlight poured through an airshaft cut into the snowy roof. It scrubbed a patch of tunnel floor a whiter white and freshened our spirits as we passed beneath it, bathed as we were momentarily in the blue sky of the outside world. I lifted my cheek to catch the faint warmth before returning to the damp. Blind Thomas only mouthed the bit and continued plodding. His big unseeing eyes were fogged with a blue gray of their own.

At last we emerged into a world that blinded me, too. Brilliant, glittering, painfully bright light shone everywhere. I shielded my face and would have waited there for my eyes to adjust, but Thomas moved tirelessly forward. A machine, he was. He well knew the routine and made a practiced half turn on the narrow and treacherously icy wagon road, then cautiously began backing the cart to the edge of the mountain's slope. I gave him the "whoa," released the catch, and watched the rocks crash downward and across the jagged faces of the previously deposited rubble.

As the echoing clamor faded, Brina sniffed the sunshine with her eyes closed and, satisfied, plopped onto her haunches. A squishy fart escaped her. She jumped up and twisted round in the air with such a comical expression of horror that I busted out laughing. And that made *me* fart. I laughed harder, doubling over even, which she took as invitation to lick my face and bounce around, all the while barking excitedly. The noise must have traveled for miles.

It was the railroad's beans that did it. There was no fresh meat to be had, so both of us were living on tinned beans and fried potatoes until the cook returned. Seems that if Mr. Sikes had any cleverness at all, he'd line us up in the tunnel immediately after supper—aiming in the proper direction, of course—and we'd have that tunnel blown through in no time.

When Brina tired of her antics and wandered off to investigate the small, white-walled clearing, I took a moment to savor the quiet. What a relief from the tunnel's nonstop pinging and pounding, its deafening crack and clatter! In all directions snow silenced the mountains beneath its blankets of white, piling them higher and thicker with each passing storm. Overhead, a pure blue sky stretched forever and ever, and I squinted upward to watch an eagle flap its broad wings.

Blind Thomas, however, wasn't enjoying the respite. Creature of habit that he was, he'd already begun fretting about this unexplained delay by vigorously swinging his head from side to side like a pendulum. "Sewing up his worries," my ma would've said.

I took a last gulp of sunshine, slammed the cart bed into place, and guided Thomas back toward the snow tunnel. Brina came trotting after us, shaking first one leg and then the other to rid her pads of packed snow. Like burrowing creatures, we returned to our dark quarters. For the winter, at least, Nature had reclaimed her territory.

Thirteen

Candlelight flickered along the rock walls, but the tunnel was unusually quiet as we returned. What was the holdup now?

We found the Chinamen encircling Ducks, who was carefully fashioning blasting cartridges from black powder and brown paper. It was time to rip away some more rock. From where I stood I could see his nimble fingers customizing the girth of each cylinder so that it would fit inside one of the narrow holes that had been drilled deep into the rock wall. These holes, a half dozen or so, pocked the upper face in a haphazard pattern, looking to me like so many smashed spiders.

His hands moved more slowly as he finished tamping the powder and sealing the cylinder openings. Envy stirred inside me. Handling explosives was the most dangerous job on the railroad construction. Ducks couldn't be more than a few years older than me. Where had he learned such skills?

Without a trace of fear he rose, climbed the scaffolding, and gently inserted each cartridge into its drilled hole. The fuse was unrolled as he climbed down. Pairs of workers then quickly dismantled the scaffolding while keeping an eye on the dangling fuses. They gave the nod to me, and I quickly led Blind Thomas and Brina out to the snow tunnel and waited there.

Thomas began fretting, of course, because we were standing still, which to his way of thinking wasn't productive work. As he swung his weight and his worry from side to side, the harness creaked in cold rhythm. Brina, on the other hand, pricked her ears and gazed back into the tunnel. None of us could see what was happening, but we all knew what was coming.

Soon enough the sound of hurrying footsteps accompanied the arrival of eleven Chinamen to the snow tunnel. We stood apart from each other, hugging ourselves against the damp cold and watching the darkened mouth of the rock tunnel for the last man, Ducks.

In that yawning silence time passed slowly, and worry began to thread my mind, as I'm sure it did theirs, too. What was taking so long? But at last came the hard patter of running footsteps, chased seconds later by an earsplitting *bang!* Blind Thomas flinched and instantly appeared annoyed at being taken by surprise. White smoke and rock dust whooshed past Ducks to envelop us all. The particles filmed our faces; they sifted inside our ears and down our collars.

I cupped my hands over Blind Thomas's nose while we waited for the air to clear. Brina, completely coated in dust, shook herself and sneezed. I thought she might sidle up to me for comfort, as she sometimes did, but to my surprise she trotted over to Ducks. He removed something from his pocket and handed it to her on his open palm. The way she took it was real easy, like she'd done it before, and that envious feeling inside me twisted into stinging jealousy. I watched him stroke her head with unguarded affection, watched her look up at him and grin.

No! Raw emotions clouded my thinking. This was wrong. Brina was *mine*.

Soon enough, she came trotting back, and when she did I left off Thomas to fondle her silky ears and scratch her neck and make a fuss over her to the point of embarrassing us both. She wriggled happily and shoved her head across my knee, stretching her honey eyes to a squint and leaving a stain of slobber. But as she spun to rub the other side of her face I saw her sneak a look over at Ducks. He was watching us, too, and half-smiling, and that hot, unsettled feeling poked at my insides. Where did Brina's loyalties lie?

The smoke was fading away now, so I got Blind Thomas turned around and we all filed our way back into the mountain. Brina, being in high spirits for some reason known only to her, loped ahead. She bounced back and forth between Ducks and me, and I could tell that the other Chinamen were talking about her. I got the sense, too, that they were teasing Ducks because of the way Brina kept returning to him. One by one they stole looks over their shoulders, gauging my reaction.

This whole situation was getting out of hand, so I whistled for her to come. She looked back, and there was a moment when she was deciding, her pink mouth spread in a wide, tongue-lolling grin. And I got more heated, because she certainly belonged to me but she wasn't coming to me. Then she winked, or blinked, I wasn't certain, and caught up to Ducks, who reached down and gave her another familiar pat on the head, and my chest got so tight it ached. The bluish half-light in the snow tunnel dimmed, like a cloud was passing over the sun, and the day got heavy. I took hold of Blind Thomas's bridle and followed.

Fourteen

I was still feeling sulky come Monday. Before our shift ended Mr. Sikes and Mr. Chang arrived together to examine our work and dispense our two weeks' pay. As promised, we were all docked for the brief work stoppage when we'd shared the soup. Mr. Sikes was still grumbling about that. And after counting out my reduced pay, he added an admonishment. "As the sole white man on this shift, Mr. Gormley, you're to keep a stricter eye on the Chinamen. They're like children," he explained, "and like children they need to be kept to do their work." Then he fished in his pocket and pulled out a small, dog-eared envelope. "This was waiting for you in Cisco. Said I'd carry it to you."

I could see it was from my ma back in New York—who'd helped her write it?—and my eyes must have grown some. That brightened the day considerably, and I felt like a squirrel with a fat acorn needing to scuttle

off and enjoy it at once. So as soon as Mr. Sikes and
Mr. Chang began sorting the pay for the Celestials, I
returned to Blind Thomas and tore it open:

My dearest Malachy,

You're living the royal life, aren't you now.
Although it be winter here and the snow a
blowing through the chinks in our walls, I
hold to my heart a vision of you in your grand
locomotive, and that teases the chill from these
poor old bones, it does. I pray to our Lord to
bless you, and I pray that you'll remember the
family who's not sharing in your bounty. But
a wee helping of the gold lining your pockets
would buy your brother and sisters and me some
flour, tea, eggs, sugar, and bread. That's all we
ask. And then it's a happy Christmas we'd be
having, indeed. I don't know when this letter may
find you, so I send along my wish that you enjoy
your Christmas Day. With all my love,

Your Ma.

I fingered the coins in my pocket, suddenly bur-
dened with guilt: My family was cold and in need of

food. With this shorted pay I had right around eighteen dollars saved, having bought a pair of new gloves and some molasses cookies a couple of weeks back from the little mercantile inside the supply car. I had to hold on to this sum for certain and mail it home as soon as I got to a town with a post office. It wouldn't arrive in time for Christmas, of course, but soon enough it would buy warmth in the form of coal, and satisfaction in the shape of a basketful of groceries.

Clink, clink, clink. Mr. Chang was dispensing the coins to his countrymen one at a time while consulting the leather-bound register balanced in the crook of his elbow. In his own language—*yut, yee, som*—he counted the money, and the pigtailed heads bobbed with each soft *clink.* They were doing their own counting, I guessed, because every so often they'd point to the sheet and then the coins in their palms and question him with heated quacking. Did they think they were being cheated?

I was rubbing Blind Thomas's forehead—he had an insatiable itch there—and thinking about Ma and Sean and Margaret and little Ellen, and what Christmas presents I'd buy for them if only I could, when, without my noticing, Ducks suddenly appeared at my side. I stiffened.

Brina the traitor—wearing the braided leather

collar I'd fashioned for her only last night to prove my ownership—bounced over for a pat. He stroked her head with one hand—and she quieted instantly—while pointing to my pocket with the other. "You have letter. I see." But it wasn't said in the same joking manner as the time he'd saved me from the falling tree.

"It's *my* letter," I said, placing my hand protectively over my pocket, though something told me he already knew that. What was up?

He looked into Brina's adoring eyes for some time, and I couldn't for the life of me tell what he was thinking. (How I wanted her to come bouncing back to *me*!) Then, out of the blue he asked, "How much you get pay?"

Huh? My pay was none of his business. Yet my pride spit out an answer: "Thirty-five a month."

That figure seemed to stab him, because he twisted his face up. Brina nuzzled his pajama pants, begging for more attention, but this time he ignored her.

"You walk out, in, out, in"—he made little scissor movements with his fingers, like they were a man's legs—"no hands dirty and company give you thirty-five?" He opened his palm, moved the coins aside, and pointed to the huge yellow calluses at the base of each finger, the juice-filled blister on his thumb, the grimed creases lining his flesh. "I hold black powder . . . drirr"—*drill*, in his clumsy accent—". . . hammer. All can kirr me. I get only thirty-one for pay." At this pronouncement I saw the midnight fire in his narrow eyes. "Why?"

My answer to that was an indifferent shrug. Black powder *was* dangerous, and it *could* kill. But he was a coolie. What did he expect?

The sound of voices and footsteps coming up the tunnel interrupted us: The night shift was hiking in. That meant it was quitting time, and my stomach rumbled in anticipation of its supper. But before I could leave, Mr. Sikes hollered, "Gormley! Haul out this load here before you put that horse away." So I began guiding Thomas into position, expecting to tell Ducks to move aside, but he'd already vanished. Sneaky as a cat, that one.

I'd returned to surliness as Thomas and I finished up. Ducks had irritated me for thinking that he deserved the same pay as I received. I was irritated with myself for not uttering the overdue thank-you and being done with it. The way Brina kept bounding over to him injured me beyond all reason. And here it was almost Christmas and my family needed what I hadn't delivered.

To announce to the world my aggravation, I suppose, I unhitched the cart at last with exaggerated sighs and let the shafts drop with a loud bang. I booted a stray rock out of the way as I coaxed Thomas forward, and it went clattering down the tunnel. Brina pricked her ears but no one else noticed. The men who were leaving were too tired to care, and the men who were arriving were strapping on their own responsibilities and concerns.

That was due to the fact that inside our tunnel there was neither day nor night and the work never ceased. While the wintry sun passed over the mountains every twenty-four hours, exchanging its blinding glitter for blue black shadows and star-filled skies, the workday inside the mountain never ended. Men labored twelve-hour shifts and then kept the candles burning so they could hand over their picks and hammers and drills to an incoming band of bleary-eyed men who took up the task of chipping away at the mountain. Such a project, we constantly reminded ourselves, had never been attempted anywhere in the world. But we were doing it, inch-by-inch, bruise-by-bruise, blister-by-blister. It seemed that the bosses could have granted a bit more leniency on the pace, but no, they wanted their tunnels dug fast and faster, cost be damned. And so our mole work went on endlessly, and whether you had the day shift or the night shift mattered only to your pocket watch.

As soon as I had Blind Thomas settled in his shed with the other two horses and chewing on his barley, Brina and I made our way to one of the cabins. The rail-road, having moved the sleeping cars to lower elevations, had hammered together a few of these winter cabins, though the structures were so flimsy that the wind pushed through the walls like they were made of cheese-cloth. It was so blasted cold inside that you never could get warmed through. Ma and I had more in common than she knew.

Workers were arriving and leaving with the chang-ing of the shifts, and the conversation was animated as Brina and I entered. "Malachy!" Patrick waved me over to where he and some others were gathered around the stove. "Come get an eyeful of Jesse's haul." Scooping a bowl of hash from the communal skillet, I went to investigate.

Jesse was seated on the ground, grinning from ear to ear like a spoiled child on Christmas morning. He looked to have robbed a mercantile, because sur-rounding him were luxuries of every kind: bundled socks, partially unwrapped sausages, and paper bags brimming with candies, as well as a small book, some nested tin plates and matching cups, a card of buttons, pouches of tobacco, and, draped across additional hid-den goods, the most beautiful paisley shawl I'd ever seen, in crimson and purple and cream. Only one thought came to mind: Ma would love to have that shawl for Christmas.

"A sutler just passed through," Patrick explained. "A

fellow on snowshoes carrying a pack bigger than he was. You just missed him."

Brina poked her head past my knee, her nose working. She spied the sausages and shot a mournful gaze up at me.

"No, there's nothing here for you, Brina," Jesse warned. But to me he said, "Since you missed the opportunity to do your Christmas shopping, I'd be willing to part with a small helping of my good fortune."

Patrick extended his feet and pointed at them. "New wool socks," he exclaimed happily. Which was something he needed, since his big toes, attached to his very big feet, were always exposed.

"Now, there's a molasses cake here somewhere," Jesse was saying, pawing his goods, "and some fine pork sausages, and well, you can have your pick of just about anything—for a price. Although," he added, fondling the beauteous scarf, and eyeing me with a polished grin, "I was planning on giving this to my mother."

That's all it took. I had to have that scarf. So before I knew it, I was paying out an extravagant eight dollars for the scarf, and then another two dollars for some dried sausages (I'd win Brina's affection come hell or high water). And when Jesse pulled a few rolls of Neccos from one of the paper bags and said they were fifty cents apiece, which I knew for a fact was robbery, well, to thank him for selling me the scarf he'd planned to give his own mother, I bought the Neccos, too. And when I carefully folded that scarf into my pack and slipped Brina a slice of sausage on the flat of my palm, just like Ducks had done, I got to feeling a whole lot better about the day and about myself.

Fifteen

When we set foot outside the cabin the next morning, the sky was still the color of gray flannel. The wind had stopped blowing after an all-night storm, and the mountains, robed in their new white, soared grandly. It was Tuesday, just another workday except for the fact that it was also Christmas Day, and that little detail turned my bunkmates and me into rascals.

Jesse started the high jinks by flinging a snowball at the back of Patrick's head, causing him to bawl like a calf. In repayment, Patrick scooped up a handful of the stuff and pitched it at Jesse. The rest of us joined in, all aiming snowballs at Jesse, until he took cover behind a tree and refused to come out; so we turned to heaving them at each other. Brina barked madly.

About that time, the Celestials emerged from their sleeping burrows—how they survived the winter's cold beneath canvas and pine boughs was beyond me—and began climbing up to the wagon road. They walked single file, their heads bowed as if in worship and their hands seeking whatever warmth had survived the night inside their padded sleeves. I didn't know which of us culprits was to blame, but a cannonball of white suddenly shot through the air and slammed into a black head. Being as it was so fresh, the snow disintegrated in a flash; I saw some of it sift inside the victim's low collar while the telltale remains splattered his shoulders. He didn't acknowledge it, just kept trudging toward the tunnel and work. Another snowball, missing its mark, shot past him and plunked into a drift. Again there was no acknowledgment.

The fun had gone, so we shrugged one to another and set off for our particular assignments. "Aye, and it's your back you'll be watching the rest of the day, Jesse Stephens," called Patrick.

"Hah! I've marked your aim, Patrick Joyce, and I'm not losing sleep over it."

Exchanging dismissive waves, they hiked in different directions. Brina and I headed for the little barn that housed the three horses working the winter with us.

For all the many mornings that I'd been fetching Blind Thomas, I almost always found him standing with his head in the corner. He wasn't sleeping; he was just waiting, lost in his woolgathering, and thus my first view of him each day was his broad black rump and chewed-on tail. Sometimes, *sometimes*, one flicking ear noted my approach, but usually he didn't respond until I began fitting his harness.

This morning, though, I entered the shelter to find that Blind Thomas had spun himself around and was facing me. As soon as he heard my footsteps he turned his unseeing eyes in my direction and nickered a welcome. And when I got closer, he shoved his head into the crook of my arm and nickered again. This alone was such a present that it warmed me through like sunshine. I patted his chest and scratched his neck and just couldn't stop smiling. I kept smiling, I think, all the way through the harnessing, not even noticing the cold that stiffened my fingers and made a difficulty of the buckling.

On our way toward the tunnel, still being in bright spirits, I spotted the tip of a small pine peeking from a windblown snowdrift. Instantly, I sized it up as being the perfect stand-in for a Christmas tree and left Thomas on the road to climb up to it. In only a couple of whacks of my axe, I was carrying it back to the dump cart, feeling like Santa Claus himself.

The Celestials working inside the tunnel gave me their cat looks, all right. "It's Christmas," I said happily, and surprised even myself by following that up with a gay

"Fa la la-la-la, la-la-la-la." I glanced toward Ducks, hoping for a friendly reaction. But his flat face, like those of his fellow workers, remained blank. "And this is a Christmas tree." My peace offering. When I held the naked sprig of greenery aloft, though, I came to see myself through their eyes: a person babbling excitedly about a wee pine when there were thousands upon thousands of the very same blanketing the mountains in every direction. That dampened my kindling somewhat.

Oh, well. I knew it was Christmas even if they didn't, and so I found a suitable crevice in the rock wall and fitted the trunk into it. Immediately, the tree twisted sideways and dangled in a limp display. That seemed to spark some amusement among them, especially when I kept setting it upright only to watch it collapse again and again. Even Ducks smiled, though he pretended not to be watching. Since my holiday spirit was rapidly evaporating, I left the troublesome bit of Christmas cheer sagging where it chose and set to work.

There was a lot of rock from the blast to be broken up and hauled off, so Blind Thomas and I had a full day ahead. It was warming into quite a pleasant one, in fact, with the morning sun climbing what was now a brilliant blue sky and only a few clouds drifting in the breeze. Because of the storm, we forged fresh tracks along the wagon path, Brina rooting through the new powder like an exuberant puppy. High above us, the white stuff towered crystalline pure and blinding.

From time to time the mountains rumbled with black powder explosions in other tunnels. And because of the warming weather, I suppose, the snow tunnel's usual damp silence was punctured by intermittent drips. But mostly the morning passed in peace, and we moved a lot of rock.

It was sometime in the afternoon, when we were emerging from the snow tunnel with another load, that Brina, always in the lead now, slowed her pace for some reason. Cocking her head, she took a few hesitant steps, sniffing like she was on to something, then came to a full stop, one paw suspended in the air. Ever so slowly, she looked back at me, her brow knitted in concern.

I sensed it too. The mountain air suddenly felt different, heavier somehow, though the sky remained a brilliant blue with no sign of a storm brewing. Even Blind Thomas, who usually marched along as steadily as a locomotive, snorted and brought the dump cart to a creaking halt behind Brina. His black ears swiveled like a pair of weathervanes as he sought to gather clues to his surroundings. But there was no enlightenment to be had. The air was just as quiet as it was heavy. Where were the birds?

Before I could ponder that question, a string of rapid

popping sounds, like decaying ice on a frozen river, ripped the air. An ominous hissing sent Blind Thomas running backward, and I had to lunge for his bridle to hold him steady. A loud rumbling began vibrating through my skin; it shook my bones and throttled my heart. The vibration built into a continual and thunderous roar, and in the blink of an eye a sheet of white swallowed up the world in front of us: a snow slide.

Brina sidled up next to my leg, and I more sensed her whimper than heard it over the all-encompassing din. Blind Thomas's hide twitched and twitched in a futile effort to shed the icy dust that was settling on his broad back.

And then it was over and the silence was more silent than before. Emptied of effort. Deflated. Dead.

I stood rooted in place, my chest heaving. What should I do? Blind Thomas started prancing, working his bit like it was chew and building into a nervous sweat. Damp patches flattened the shaggy hairs on his neck and belly, and a greenish foam bubbled at his lips.

I had to see what damage the snow slide had done, so I tugged on his bridle. He took a reluctant step forward, then braced his knee like he was planting it in one spot. I tugged again. "Come along, Thomas," I urged. He flicked an ear and took one more stiff, marionette step, clearly not wanting any part of this venture. I kept coaxing him along, though, fighting for each step, and Brina accompanied me at the same tentative pace. Her wet nose was twitching like a fidgety rabbit's.

We made it down the curving snow-packed wagon road toward the edge of the slide, and if you didn't know what had just happened, you'd think nothing at all had changed. The blue sky still arched across an endless vista of mountains and pines. White snow still covered the slopes. But I saw that everything had changed. The huge swath of snow that had broken off the mountain above and come crashing down in a giant wave had buried everything in its path. The road we were on. The trees. A cabin.

Oh, Jesus, Mary, and Joseph! One of the cabins had been picked up and floated downhill like it was a toy. It rested now at a dizzying angle, half-buried in the debris, and I could hear the desperate holler of at least one man who was trapped inside.

Abandoning Thomas, I went racing back inside the mountain, Brina loping at my side. "Help!" I yelled, and twelve faces lifted. "There's been a snow slide!" I made a big sweeping movement with my arm. They exchanged quizzical looks, so I spoke directly to Ducks and repeated the pantomime. "A snow slide! Come quick!" I implored. Ducks threw down his pick and said something to his mates. Gesturing for them to follow, I sprinted back through the tunnel with Brina. Behind us, tools clattered to the ground, and thumping footsteps sounded hard on our heels.

I raced all the way down the rock tunnel and through the blue half-light of the snow tunnel and then out onto the sunlit wagon road.

But I didn't see Blind Thomas. He wasn't where I'd left him. Oh, God!

I could hardly breathe, but I kept charging forward. My heart hammered as I shielded my eyes and squinted against the blinding drifts. Finally, when I reached the curve, I spotted him. He was farther along the wagon road, floundering in the chest-high white stuff. He'd followed our routine and, in trudging onward, gotten himself disoriented amid the snow slide's debris. Now he was trying with great effort to back the dump cart to the edge of the down slope and was closer than he realized: One wheel already wobbled at the precipice.

"Thomas!" I hollered. "Whoa!" I waded toward him, working my arms and straining to pump my knees against the white muck that fought me. "Whoa! Whoa!" Icicles stabbed my lungs. *"Whoa!"*

Obedient animal that he was, Thomas finally halted in his tracks. His neck stretched high and stiff, though, and his ears were pinned to his head, so annoyed was he at this confusing predicament. I was almost to him when the cart's wheel lost some traction and the granite load we'd been moving shifted with a threatening clatter. The cart's twisting frame squealed. "Steady, lad!" I called.

And then I had my fingers on his bridle, urgently tugging him forward. He leaned into the effort and pulled the cart away from the drop-off. The rocks rumbled anew. My hands were shaking—hell, my entire body was shaking—but when we'd moved safely away from the drop-off, I managed to lift one palm to his neck. He was trembling too, poor creature.

Ducks and the others were already organizing a rescue effort, so I split my attention between Blind Thomas and them. A rope was brought forth and, once the end was knotted around his waist, a volunteer was lowered, half-crawling and half-sliding, down the snow-foamed mountainside.

We all watched as individuals from the night shift, men I didn't know by name, clambered out of the capsized cabin. Each in turn fitted the rope around his own waist and was pulled, half-crawling and half-stumbling, up to safety. Once they were all returned, the volunteer Chinaman was also pulled upward.

"That's a fine wake-up call!" one of the rescued men exclaimed. Gingerly, he touched a hand to his bruised cheek.

"Fine it was," said another, blinking wildly. "Woke

me up but good." His hair stood at all angles and his jaw-bone was streaked with blood, though he didn't seem to be aware of it.

The men were all accounted for, apparently, but here were Ducks and the others lowering the same volunteer down the slope again at the end of the rope. Why?

I glanced past the edge, and a sick realization kicked my gut. The snow slide had also swept over and obliterated the Chinamen's winter burrows. The men sleeping there had had no wooden structure, however flimsy, for protection, and the torrent of snow had obviously crushed them where they lay. There wasn't a solitary sign of them now, not a flailing hand, not a pigtail, not a snow-tossed teacup. They were gone. Just like that, a whole pack of Celestials—why didn't I know how many?—were gone.

"Hey, now," hollered one of the rescued men. He and a comrade shoved Ducks and his mates out of the way and yanked the rope into their own hands. They started reeling it upward though the Celestial dangling on the slope below squawked in protest.

"You're gonna get yourself killed with such foolishness!" In a few powerful jerks they had him topside. "Now, go on about your business," one man ordered, unfastening the rope and shooing away the would-be rescuer like he was an insect. "There's nothing to be done for those that are down there," he chided. "You couldn't even dig 'em out with shovels. Snow's too deep." He coiled the rope, dropped it on the ground, and stomped back toward his dazed companions.

In his wake the little cluster of blue-jacketed men crept close to the slope's edge to gaze down forlornly at the deadly swath of white.

Sixteen

Things got solemn after that. The rescued men, along with the newly homeless Celestials, piled into the two remaining cabins, and the tight spaces shortened all our fuses. Living right on top of one another, I got a firsthand look at the peculiarities of Ducks and his countrymen.

First, of course, was their round-the-clock tea drinking. They had to have a pot of it simmering at all times and, since the cooking fire was outside, one of them was constantly climbing to his feet and slipping through the door to dip his cup. And with each coming and going a wintry gust scattered our playing cards, bit our cheeks, and otherwise poked our tempers.

Second was their bathing. Bathing! Why anyone would willingly strip off his clothes in the middle of winter to sit naked in a barrel of water was beyond my ken.

But at the end of our shift—and, mind you, it was as dark as pitch by that hour—each and every one of those pig-tailed little men, including Ducks, would have his turn at it. My bunkmates rolled their eyes at the nightly parade.

"Like a bunch of women!" muttered Patrick.

"It ain't natural, that's for dang sure," added Jesse, laying down two pair and collecting his winnings.

I was in full agreement. It was flat-out wrong to take such a strong and regular interest in soaping up your body. Just picturing the goings-on right outside the cabin walls, in fact, gave me a case of the allovers. It was affecting my card playing, and the gold I was supposed to send to my family was again going fast.

Money—pretend money, that is—was also slipping through the slender fingers of Ducks and his mates. I watched early one morning as they scoured the camp for unwanted papers only to tear them into strips and toss them onto a fire. Sitting on their heels, they solemnly watched the clouds of smoke drift upward. "Money for grandparents," Ducks explained, when he noticed me hovering. "Money for eight men lost in snow slide. They need in spirit world." I found myself standing there and nodding, as if I actually believed such nonsense.

There were the strange foods, of course, slimy bits of pungent greens and oily tinned fishes, all tossed with the rice that prevailed at every meal. And the two slim sticks they used in place of a regular knife and fork. But strangest of all were their Sunday habits—which sometimes began as early as Saturday night, since we didn't work the next day. The Celestials, you see, instead of lifting a glass or two, smoked their opium.

That seemed like another feminine art, because they had to help each other get the job done. One held the long wood and silver pipe to his mouth while the other heated a pellet of opium in its tiny bowl. A spitting and fizzing erupted as the opium burned, followed by a gurgle indicating the pipe was delivering its enjoyment. The instrument was handed from one to another, and soon a sickeningly sweet aroma, like too many crushed flowers, filled the room.

Jesse would combat the perfume by passing out cigars, and we'd sit puffing with such earnestness and such abandon that a blue cloud of smoke thicker than any fog swirled inside our cabin. After a while, my eyes burned like they were on fire, my mind got fuzzy, and I could hardly make out the bunks on the opposite wall.

On nights such as these the peculiar, choppy language of the Chinamen huddled in the corner melted into murmurs. Long silences eventually knitted the gaps between their contented sighs. Glancing over my shoulder now and then, and blinking hard, I saw a haphazard pile of blue-clad arms and legs, all entangled with slumping shoulders and lolling heads. Smiles lit their golden faces. Sometimes their feet paddled in the way a dog does when he's dreaming, and it occurred to me that this was about the only time I'd seen them happy.

Were they dreaming about their homes, about their families? Were they planning what they'd do with all the gold they were earning?

Or was this a different sort of happiness, the kind that comes when you realize things can't possibly get any worse? Was their drug-addled joy merely a numbing to the pain of their friends' deaths?

That was some serious thinking that could get me to feeling bad and make me miss my ma and brother and sisters. Remembering the day my pa had marched off to the war, chanting and whooping loudly with the others in the Sixty-ninth, the Fighting Irish, only to get himself killed that first month, twisted a knife into my side all over again.

So on nights such as those I'd look over my shoulder at the sleeping Celestials and try to count the smiles. Maybe that's what opium was good for. It lightened the load we all carried. At least for a day.

It snowed again the following night, inches upon inches, feet upon feet. And it kept snowing right on into January. Such miserable weather didn't keep Ducks and his mates from choosing to move out of our cabin, though.

Using only scraps of sawn lumber and tree branches, they fashioned a series of rickety frameworks along the leeward side of the horse shed, then draped canvas over the whole enterprise. Snow piled atop the sagging shelters, but they cooked and ate and slept beneath the drifts, happily living like animals again. Peculiar, indeed.

Winter storms continued rolling through. Snow fell steadily through January and February, and March alone piled another ten feet on top of the white drifts that already engulfed us. You couldn't see anything of the crumpled cabin by then. Its remains had been laid to rest and buried, along with the bodies of the Celestials, under a thick, silent blanket of white. Supplies, as well as the gold coins we were earning, couldn't reach us and piled up elsewhere.

And each new workday, we hiked back into the tunnel.

Seventeen

Early in April, Mr. Chang managed to arrive on snow-shoes, and if that wasn't ever a sight. The little man was the Celestial coming of Santa Claus with his bulging sack of tinned and dried foodstuffs, tissue-wrapped clothing (all sewn of blue cotton), several folded newspapers, and—of all things—a colorful paper kite. Ducks took possession of the kite but seemed more excited about the newspapers. As soon as Mr. Chang departed, he sat reading aloud while he fashioned blasting cartridges—which, to my mind, was a very dangerous thing to do and showed his carelessness. But by then I was itching so badly for news that I listened to the choppy language anyway, though with growing envy, since I had no idea what they were sharing.

When Ducks came strolling past for his tea break, I busied myself fastening the feed bag around Blind

Thomas's head. Brina, of course, wriggled in excitement and rose up to greet him, but I stamped on the rope that served as her leash now, and she came up short.

Eight odd-looking coins had been sewn across the chest of his padded jacket—odd-looking because they were unusually sized and had square holes cut into their centers. Chinese coins, I assumed. Mother of God, did he have so much money he could ornament his clothing with it? Studiously ignoring him, I brushed the dust from Blind Thomas's broad back, then picked up his huge feet one by one to demonstrate my skill with the big animal.

Ducks squatted with his tea and unfolded one of his newspapers, paying me no mind. Sooner than I'd like to admit, of course, curiosity nudged me to peer over his shoulder. Scarce bit of good that did, since the page was covered in the tiniest of ink scratches rather than proper letters. Still . . .

"What's the news?" I asked, casual, like I didn't really care.

His narrow eyes passed over Brina on her leash, then lifted to me, flashing emotion. "Man work for Hop Sing Company. Other man in La Porte—*not* Chinese—shoot him for land he own. Land he *own!*" Stabbing at the scratches, he added, "Now he dead."

"My pa was killed in the war." Instantly I wished I

could take back those words. What did they have to do with the dead Chinese man?

Of course, he stared at me like I was a blathering idiot.

"Are you from La Porte?" I asked.

Frowning, he slapped his chest and said, "From Kwangtung province."

Sounded like he was gargling with those syllables. "In China?"

"China, yes. I come on boat with uncle, work for railroad. He save moneys, send for wife. I no have wife. I save moneys."

Took me a few blinks to follow the winding thread of that one. "For a wife?"

He shrugged. The hint of a smile, sly and catlike, settled across his face. "Maybe. If many moneys, then many wives."

Many moneys, huh? Just how much was *many moneys*, and would they replenish what I'd been losing at cards? Because I now owed Jesse more than a month's wages.

Stop. You stop that thinking this instant, Malachy Gormley. Why was it that such mind scolding always came in my ma's voice? *'Tis sinful thinking, that is.*

Feeling heat crawl up my neck, I tugged my thoughts away from the imagined heap of coins. I shunned the empty feel to my pockets, ignored the itch in my right palm that said those coins could—perhaps should—be in my hand.

I don't know why I was being so talkative, but out of curiosity I asked, "What was your name again?"

"Chun Kwok Keung." Which, as before, came out like the quacking of so many ducks.

Then, to my surprise, he shot to his feet and politely responded, "What your name, please?" In abrupt after-thought he extended his hand.

"Malachy Gormley." And although I glanced at the thin little hand, I didn't clasp it. So he dropped it to his side, looking a little ashamed, and sank onto his heels. That heat started crawling up my neck again. Pointing to the coins with the square holes that he had sewn to his coat, I asked, "What are those?"

One by one he fingered the coins thoughtfully. "For remember eight mens die when . . ." Searching for the word, he made a sweeping movement with his arm that I instantly recognized.

"Snow slide? Your friends who were buried in the snow slide?"

He nodded, and the way he held his finger on the last coin, sort of stroking it, got to me. As he squatted there, traveling through memories with his lost friends, I real-ized that I still couldn't tell his age for certain. Seventeen?

Twenty-one? Although his face was smooth, with only a hint of something shadowy above his lip, it was as tanned as polished saddle leather. To my surprise I saw that his eyes weren't black, as I'd first thought but, rather, a deep oily brown. His hair was blue black, though, as dark as printer's ink, and so fine that what strands weren't caught up in the braid running along his back fringed his forehead and swept his knobby cheekbones.

When his gaze fell on Brina, she started wriggling again and straining at the end of her rope. I tugged her backward. "Sit!" I ordered. She did, reluctantly, all the while looking from him to me and back again. Then, giving out a mournful whine, she dropped to the ground and rested her head on her paws.

"Why?" Ducks indicated Brina with an open palm. "Why 'sit'?"

"Because she belongs to me."

I don't know if he understood that or not. But his black brows knitted together in somewhat of a frown, and Brina's tail thumped hopefully. He jerked his chin toward Blind Thomas. "He sit?"

Oh, good Lord. Who was the idiot now? "No," I said crossly, "horses don't sit."

"Because no belong?"

I threw up my hands. "Time for you to get to work." And for some reason I remembered the scene back in

Cisco when the cutups across the street had been aping Mr. Strobridge. I'd learned since then that the Celestials were terrified of the one-eyed man's fiery temper as well as of the pick handle he carried at the ready, so I covered an eye and brought my fist slashing through the air. "Chinaman needs to work! Chop-chop! Chop-chop!"

He slowly unfolded himself, and Brina rose up with him, arranging her haunches and eyeing me with that cool, royal look she could pull out of thin air. Ducks bowed his head in stiff acknowledgment. "Gorm *Li*?" he said as he gathered his newspaper. "Li is Chinese name. You work also, *di-di*." And he walked ramrod straight into the tunnel.

I watched him go with a queer feeling roiling around inside me. The nervy little scoundrel had no business speaking to me like that, and I was fairly hot about it. But here was Brina, her golden eyes brimming with disdain, which bothered me, and when I turned around, even Blind Thomas—the animal with no sight at all—had his head craned in my direction. His ears flicked forward and back in vexation. "What?" I growled, and sent a chunk of granite clattering across the ground with my boot, which startled both creatures. Feeling no better at all, I resumed brushing Blind Thomas with such furious energy that he sidled out from beneath the brush first one way and then the other until I softened my strokes.

My path didn't cross Ducks's the rest of that workday, and a good thing, too. But after I'd returned Blind Thomas to his shed that evening and Brina and I were making our way through the trees over to the cabin, I spotted the silhouette of a man higher up on the wagon road. The snow-covered slopes behind him glistened in the fading light, showing him to be a Celestial. I knew it had to be Ducks.

He was sending up a kite, the one Mr. Chang had delivered, and the sharp wind buffeted the colorful contraption against a sheet of lavender sky. Ducks began working that kite with full concentration, pacing back and forth, feeding out line then tugging it back in. And as the kite swooped and soared like a joyous, flapping bird, I saw that a string of tiny candlelit paper lanterns was fastened to its tail. The starlike flames danced in the twilight. I couldn't help myself: I stood mesmerized.

When the wind changed direction and swept down the slope past me, I realized that Ducks was singing. It was a plaintive song of loss, of a lonesome soul in mourning. Of course I couldn't understand the words, but the keening melody unexpectedly picked me up and swept me with the force of a gale wind back to that distant New York port, where my fingers once again gripped the rail of a ship that was drifting steadily away from the dock. Green gray waves multiplied upon each other, stretching longer and longer between me and the teary face of my ma trying to elbow her way forward through the crowd. My throat got that choky feeling then, and I turned away, preparing to walk off, but here was Brina planted beside me and gazing skyward, something I'd never seen a dog do; and I got the impression she wasn't going to move. So I turned back and waited and kept watching.

One by one, stars poked through the twilight and the tiny lanterns on Ducks's kite greeted them with a twirling frenzy. They shivered and spun, and bobbed up and down on their string. And then came another unexpected occurrence: I laughed! It wasn't a big laugh, not the kind of roar that comes at the end of a good joke, but more a chuckle of approval, one that warmed me through to the inside. It felt so right that I held its echoing smile on my lips until my cheeks numbed. Reaching down, I fondled Brina's ears and rubbed her neck, happy to be sharing the sight with her. This was one of those moments, I realized, when the world seems to hold its breath and pry open your eyes to the way of things. *'Tis a rare and unusual event, Malachy,* I'd heard my ma say often enough. *Stand up and take notice.* I did so and counted it a blessing.

Then the singing ended. Ducks pulled the string gently, and the lanterns answered with rippling nods. He brought them round again, almost in an embrace, then swept his arm upward and released the kite and its little beacons of light—all eight of them—into the night sky.

A sudden gust snatched up the contraption and carried it out of sight; and I was still smiling, though getting a wee bit choky again. But seeing those eight little lanterns strive for the heavens made me feel that, at least for the moment, all was right with the world. 'Twas a good feeling, that, letting go.

Eighteen

June came, and though the weather warmed and the mountains turned green, the snow still lay ten feet deep in some ravines. The forests livened with frolicking creatures. Noisy squirrels played chase up and down tree trunks, taking dizzying leaps between branches that soared over breakneck slopes. In the canopy, woodpeckers echoed our hammering with their own busy work. Winging through sun and shadow, and calling incessantly, were the black-and-white magpies. I watched them stashing their treasures in the litter of the forest floor and envied their bounty.

That's because I'd gotten myself into an awful mess with my card playing. I'd even tried selling Ma's Christmas scarf back to Jesse to help cover my losses, but he wouldn't take it. "Can't buy fencing with scarves, Malachy. I'll be requiring the gold." And he made a mark on the little piece of paper he kept folded in his pocket. I was growing desperate.

Then came one Saturday evening that we'd had to put in extra hours, so it was dark by the time I emerged from getting Blind Thomas settled in his shed. All I wanted to do was spoon some supper into my belly and climb into my bunk, but here were Ducks and two of his mates pointing up at the stars and chattering about something. Thoroughly out of sorts, I looked up.

"That is Cowboy over there, and that is Weaver Girl," Ducks explained, indicating two especially bright stars. "They are"—he paused, searching for the right word—"lonely. All the year kept apart by silver river." Again he pointed toward the sky.

"That's the Milky Way," I said.

He only blinked one of his owl blinks at me and, with his two mates listening as well, talked on. "One day each year, ten thousand magpies fly into sky. Make bridge so two lovers can meet. Only one time each year. Next morning they must part. Rain always follows: Weaver Girl's tears."

Was he funnin' me? Because I wasn't in the mood.

"Tomorrow," he said with a confident nod, "is that day." His friends concurred with their own nods, which made fools of all three of them. Fed up with such nonsense, I waved them off and, shaking my head, strode toward the cabin.

But the following morning, Sunday, when I first set foot outside, I was surprised to discover that the forest lay oddly quiet. A lone squirrel looked down at me from a tree limb, twitching his tail and seeming nervous. And in the distance the stream babbled across its rocks; but there were no other sounds and no morning bird songs. The hairs on the back of my neck stirred as I searched the branches, the mountain slopes, the open sky. Where were the magpies?

Odd thing was, up until that morning the noisy black-and-white nuisances had been everywhere, stealing food scraps right off your plate or flitting away with a popped rivet or broken buckle or anything that caught the sunlight. I saw a magpie once manage to fly off with a fork in his beak, his wings barely clearing the needle-carpeted ground. They were, truly, as thick as thieves.

But now they seemed to have vanished. Not so much as a feather drifted earthward.

Ducks emerged from his sleeping quarters to stretch and give a wave of acknowledgement. "Tonight they meet," he called. Then he began puttering around his camp, gathering up plates and buckets and jars. And humming. "Tonight they meet," he called again when Patrick and Jesse joined me outside. I'd already informed them of Ducks's prognostication, so they rolled their eyes. "They hug. They kiss. They are together," he said happily. We sauntered off toward our coffee.

I wasn't in the habit of lingering near the Chinamen's camp; none of us were. But as the day wore on, being curious about Ducks's activities, some of us strolled closer to the ramshackle community of canvas-draped dwellings.

For that one afternoon, at least, the ridicule we often heaped on the Celestials was shelved. It had been a long, quiet day, boring even, and I think we were all feeling lonely enough that we wanted to believe in Ducks's tale of lovesick stars coming together in the sky. We wanted to believe in the promise of reunion, cling to the hope that we hadn't been forgotten the many months we'd been separated from our families. I know I sat on my heels thinking about my ma and my brother and sisters, wondering when I'd see them again.

We watched Ducks busy himself setting out pots and saucers and tin cups, anything to catch the promised rain. It was a very special rain, he informed us, good for healing. I looked up at the clear sky: not a chance.

I wasn't the only one. Several of the men had already laid their wagers against it—though not any Chinamen, which was unusual, because they'd bet on *anything*, even something as random as which flower a bee might land on. Jesse, of course, was taking the bets and holding the money. If he noticed the odds, Ducks wasn't bothered; he just kept humming and smiling.

We watched and chatted and exchanged stories right up until suppertime. When clouds crept in at dusk, obscuring the stars, it began to look like Ducks might be right about the rain, but I, for one, was a little saddened that we wouldn't be able to witness his once-a-year miracle. Soon enough the deepening mountain cold sent us trudging back to our cabin.

Rain did fall during the night, a real soaking rain, though that wasn't the biggest surprise. By midmorning Ducks had sold—*sold!*—that water to his fellow Chinamen, those that hadn't set out their own cups and plates, anyway. He claimed it to be healing water. Pour on burn, he promised, no pain. Drink it down, no stomach sickness. Once-a-year special water. Only at a special price. He pocketed a small fortune in gold that day. All from water. All from selling hope.

Nineteen

By the end of that month we were pushing so deep into the mountain that we could often hear the team on the opposite side tunneling toward us. Muffled explosions sent vibrations traveling beneath our feet. We lit fuses and sprinted, answering with rattling thunderclaps of our own.

To spur us on, Mr. Sikes offered a week's pay to each man on the team that first tunneled the next fifteen feet of rock. That was more than a little enticing until I learned from the men in the cabin that the race was highly unfair, that we were teamed mostly with Chinese, while the other, unseen, team was composed wholly of Irish grit and brawn. There was no way we could win. The Celestials were steady workers, it was true, but slow; nothing could set a fire under them. So, really, what was the point of us breaking our backs?

I never heard mention of the prize after that and assumed the other team had won it.

With the snow melting, the mail started to arrive again, and I received not one but two letters from my ma, which seemed an extravagance of postage, and then an alarm went off that something was dreadfully wrong at home. I nearly ripped the letters in half in my rush to get them open, only to read the same litany as the one that had been preached to me back in December.

Ye must be living like royalty now and have forgotten your poor family who are left behind in this miserable city. But we haven't forgotten you, Malachy. Every morning I bend these old knees to the cold floor and I pray to God to bless my firstborn and keep him safe. Protect him, I pray, from the thieves who will try to get to that money that'll be lining his pockets. 'Tis a lovely thing to have all the bounty of Heaven bestowed upon you, Malachy, but remember little Ellen, who's growing out of her only dress, and your brother, Sean, who's scrubbing the tables at the Fair Dublin after hours and could surely use a set of snug boots to keep the snow from his toes. As for your dear ma, all I ask is your remembrance.

The second letter was brief:

Your sister Margaret took a tumble down the
back stairs and broke her arm. The doctor's
bill is $4.25. We don't have the money. Please,
Malachy, don't forget us.

Those words tied a lead weight around my heart
and sank it to my stomach. I crumpled the papers and
stuffed them into my pocket, noting with a stab of guilt
the lack of gold coins there. I was supposed to be taking
my pa's place and supporting my family. But I was failing
at that, as my ma was pointing out to me. Why couldn't I
hold on to enough of my pay to send to them?

Some of the Celestials had received letters, too,
including Ducks. I expected him to whoop with joy—
hadn't he been waiting months for this?—but he stood as
still as a statue just holding the letter in his hand. One of
his mates finally said something to him and only then did
Ducks begin to unseal the envelope, taking his own time
with the wax closure. He couldn't have read the entire
letter in the brief glance he gave it before he let it drift to
the tunnel floor. With no emotion at all on his marble face
he picked up his hammer and returned to work.

Seemed a low day for both of us, waiting on news
and then being delivered a packet of disappointment or

guilt or—who knew—maybe even betrayal or loss. Sure made the rock heavier.

The following week the railroad dangled another prize. Mr. Sikes and Mr. Chang arrived together to announce that the railroad had decided to give the Chinese workers a four-dollar-a-month raise, lifting their pay to thirty-five dollars a month. But they'd have to put in a longer day, Mr. Chang added, at least ten hours.

"He work more hours?" Ducks said, pointing to me. I got heated at once.

"No. This has nothing to do with him," Mr. Sikes jumped in. "The offer from the Central Pacific Railroad Company—a very generous offer, I might add—is for Chinese laborers only. You won't match those wages anywhere." When he smiled, his coffee-stained dentures peeked from beneath a bushy moustache of the same color.

The Celestials exchanged looks and, without saying a word to one another, began shaking their heads.

"Don't you understand?" Mr. Sikes implored. "You'll be getting paid the same as the white men. That's an exceptional offer."

"But work more hours."

"Well, you don't expect a salary for nothing, do you? This isn't a charity we're operating."

Ducks scowled. "*Now* work more hours," he said firmly. "*And* buy food. *And* sleep in dirt. Not same as him." Again a finger was pointed in my direction. Why? I had nothing to do with this.

Right away their foreman, Mr. Chang, spoke sharply in the native gibberish, but rather than silence Ducks the rebuke loosed a torrent of caterwauling. Next thing you knew, the two were face-to-face, hissing and spitting like tomcats. Their whiny nonsense words ran up and down the scale and tumbled right off. Knotting around the pair, the other Chinamen added to the clamoring chorus; then Ducks drew himself tall, clamped his mouth shut, and folded his arms. He was finished. Turning to Mr. Sikes, he stated, "Work *eight* hours. *Forty* dollars."

The man drew back as if he'd been slapped. He shot a glare at Mr. Chang, then spluttered, "What? What did you—why, you can't negotiate with *me*! This offer isn't open to negotiation. You'll accept the conditions or you'll accept your severance. I'll have you know I can replace each and every one of you like *that*!" And he snapped his fingers no more than an inch in front of Ducks's nose.

I have to say I admired that Ducks didn't so much as blink. His face remained stone cold, though anyone who was looking could see that his eyes burned with a black fire. "Eight hours, forty dollars," he said calmly.

"Never!" Mr. Sikes turned on the Chinese foreman. "You'd better fit some muzzles on these coolies of yours, Chang. I'll not be subjected to such insolence." And he

stormed out of the tunnel, leaving Mr. Chang to fall victim to the flock of black-pigtailed crows that descended
upon him with their cackling anger.

As for me, I hurriedly shoveled the last of the rock
onto the dump cart, and Blind Thomas and Brina and I
stepped lively away from the bickering countrymen.

With the push to punch through the mountain
renewed, the railroad sent up more workers, and some
of them moved into our cabin.

One of them was a man only a few years older than
me by the name of Collin Ruddy. He had a friendly way
about him, and I liked him right off, especially since he
admired Brina.

"Ace dog, that," he said the first evening when he
was settling onto his bunk. I was fooling with a deck of
cards, extending my own agony since the game was over
and my pockets had once again been emptied. "She a
fighter?"

Swelling with pride, I gave Brina a couple of hearty
claps on the chest. "She can hold her own," I replied,
remembering how she'd taken on the other dogs in the
alley in Sacramento.

"I got a dog back home," he said. "Name of Maccon.
Won some money fighting him, I'll tell ye."

I gazed down at Brina with a fresh eye. My pa would
have loved owning a fighting dog. Maybe he would have

been proud of me, too, for owning Brina. He might have paraded the both of us down to the brewery even, bragging on us and exaggerating our accomplishments. He might have.

As if she could hear the path my thoughts were traveling, Brina lifted her eyes up to me. Her solemn expression said no.

Well, it was something to think about, Ellen needing a new dress and all, and Sean nearly barefoot. And the doctor with his hand sticking out.

The door to the cabin stood open then because the weather was mild, and looking through it we saw the Celestials going about their bathing.

"They're a queer folk, now, aren't they?" Collin flashed a conspiratorial grin. "Sure and I'd heard tales of them before sailing west, but what a sight! Mincing all about San Francisco, they were; as fine a gaggle of ladies as you ever saw, wearing their blue nightshirts in the high sun and their basket hats upside down."

He had an energetic way of chewing his tobacco while he spoke that put me in mind of a cow dreading a thunderstorm; that's how hard he was working that plug of his. Regular streams of brown juice arced in the direction of the bucket sitting at the cabin's entry but splattered instead on the wall behind it and on the floor. Patrick would be frowning at that.

"But I don't pay them any mind," Collin continued. "My religion is, they don't truck with me and I don't truck with them." He banged his boot on the floor before unlacing it, which sent a little spray of sand tinkling against the wall. "Not that I've lost so much as a wink about it, because I don't believe there's a one of them could square up to a real fight." Another brown rainbow shot through the air. "There was this one time back in San Francisco when I saw two of them quarreling; looked like a pair of schoolgirls jumping up and down, they did, their braids flying, squawking like chickens getting their tail feathers pulled. But I'm telling ye, neither of them ever threw a punch. Why, I'd wager a solid gold dollar if you put a fist up to one of their slant-eyed mugs—not connect, mind ye—why, I'd wager they'd just about faint flat out cold with fear." His hooting laughter brought Brina to her feet. She looked at him, then at me. Assured there was no need for alarm, she planted her rump but fixed her attention on this newcomer.

Ducks hurried past the door at that moment. Collin watched him go and then, even though he was in his stocking feet, whispered, "Watch this!" and went traipsing out the door in the direction of the water barrel that served as the Celestials' tub. They'd suspended a rope between two trees and had hung a blanket across it for privacy. This rope was also where they hung their clothes while they were naked in the water. I moved to the door as Collin tiptoed across the ground and silently removed the blue cotton clothing. He came running back with it, giggling like a kid. A yelp sounded from behind the blanket.

"What do ye say?" Collin asked, swinging the clothing around his head. "Let her fly?"

I shook my head. Ducks was howling blue murder, and I felt for him. "Hang it back up," I said.

Performing a mocking bow, Collin replied, "As you wish." He first made a show of "accidentally" dropping the clothing in the dirt, then picked up the garments and tossed them high in the branches of a nearby cedar. Then he sat himself in the doorway and waited. Wasn't long before Ducks climbed out of his bath and shot past us, his hands cupped low. He was wearing nothing but his pigtail and a heavy load of shame. Some of that shame splashed onto me before I could slink back inside the cabin.

Twenty

The first thing I saw upon stepping outside the cabin on a workday morning late in June was a couple dozen of the Celestials lingering beside their cooking fire, lazing like it was a Sunday. Almost to a man they were watching the goings-on of that peculiar gambling game, the one with the cup and the dried beans. Squawks and yelps marked their play. Why weren't they heading to their work?

Even more odd was that another of them was boldly hiking off toward the stream with a fishing pole balanced on his shoulder, and yet another was methodically string- ing a hammock between two trees, obviously intending to nap. The malingerer.

Where was Ducks? He had a hand in this. I knew that as surely as I knew that Mr. Sikes was going to have his hide and all their yellow hides for not taking up their hammers and drills. I scanned the strange scene again, but as far as I could tell Ducks was nowhere in sight.

Oh, well, I didn't really care a rap about their unusual mischief. I had my own work to tend to, and so I set off with Brina toward the horses' shed in order to harness Blind Thomas for the day. That was a task I looked forward to each and every morning, a task that popped me out of my bunk no matter the weather, and it was wholly due to that horse's greeting.

All right, I'd gone soft, admittedly—soft to the point of red-faced mortification if anyone were to learn how much I looked forward to his morning welcome. But I did; his call made me feel special, and already I was listening to my boots crunch on the gritty path, knowing he was listening too. Any second now he'd release an enthusiastic nicker that started deep inside his chest and rippled up the scale like dawn's trumpet, quickening my heart and my step.

And then the loony depths of my affection for this horse would be further revealed. Because I'd begun answering Blind Thomas in his own language. Meaning that, yes, I whinnied back.

Casually now I glanced over my shoulder to make certain the path was empty; I was taking no chances of being found out. Patrick and Jesse and now Collin were always looking to lord the advantage over someone exposing a weakness, the most recent example of that having occurred one night last week. Ethan was back, and he'd been feeling low because he missed cradling his infant son, hadn't seen him in weeks, he moaned. So what did Patrick do? In the dark hours before sunrise he fashioned a bib around his neck and planted himself in Ethan's lap, wailing to raise the devil and waking us all, just like an infant.

Precisely because of those pranksters, I made a point of being the last one to the horse shed each morning so I could have my time with Blind Thomas in private. It was the best part of my day. I could tell that horse anything and everything, unburden myself as it were, like going to confession—though I'd never enjoyed going to confession back in New York and wasn't at all certain that Father Maguire kept my sins to himself. But Blind Thomas did. He loosened my tongue like no human ever had, and he never once betrayed my trust.

Why wasn't he calling? I could hear him shuffling about inside the shed. Was he waiting for me to go first? Okay. I opened my mouth, took a deep breath, and released a belly-tightening whinny that pulsed like a real horse's cry.

No response. Oh, Lord, something was wrong!

Jogging the last steps up to the door, I was surprised

to find that someone had left it unlatched. That was odd, but I didn't have time to ponder it, because Brina shoved past my knees, knocking me against the door frame. What in the Sam Hill was her hurry?

Soon enough I saw: It was Ducks. And he'd no doubt heard me just now making a fool of myself, which set me on edge. The trespasser was standing in front of Blind Thomas, awkwardly rubbing my horse's forehead with the heel of his hand like they were the best of friends. Obviously he knew nothing about horses, yet Blind Thomas was beginning to let his lower lip sag in the pleasurable stupor he got into when I groomed him. Of course Brina bounded through the bedding like a puppy, and that startled Thomas, who lifted his head and snorted. Ducks said something in his own quacking, then bent down to play-wrestle with her.

"What are you doing here?" I demanded.

The confident smile he delivered irritated me. "You talk to horse; I want talk to horse." He ruffled Brina's neck, then shrugged. "But horse no talk."

Her leap upward to lick his face elicited a laugh, and he doubled the vigor of his play with her, slapping her chest and stroking her neck and doing everything he could to pamper her. Like I wasn't doing enough of that.

"Brina, come!" I ordered. She ignored me. Pretended like she was deaf in the way Thomas was blind. "Brina! *Brina, come!*"

That timber-rattling shout finally took the air out of her, and she came slinking over. I patted her head and rubbed her ears in nearly the same manner as Ducks, and after a time she collapsed her weight against my leg with a grunt. Her lips drew back in a panting grin, a grin she seemed to be sharing with Ducks and not me, and that made me more irritated. I shifted my resentment to him. "You don't belong here. Why aren't you working?"

"Strike." The word was tossed matter-of-factly, arrogant in its simplicity.

"Strike? You can't strike."

He spread his palms—*What do you think I'm doing?*—and his black eyebrows rose in speechless retort. As I said: arrogant.

"Why? The railroad's offering you four dollars a month more."

He inclined his head. "Yes. Thirty-five dollar good for white man. Now forty-five dollar good for China man."

"Forty-five?" Brina's eyes swung up to me. "You can't get forty-five. That's more than us."

He shrugged. "We work more hours. Work more hard." His flat face glowed with an inner excitement.

Returning his attentions to Blind Thomas, he began making small circles on the horse's neck with his knuckles. "Must teach respect," he said. "Always teach respect."

Who knew what that gibberish was supposed to mean? "It won't do any good. You think just because you and a couple of your mates refuse to work today that the railroad won't boot you off this mountain and send for other Chinamen?"

"No China man work."

"What do you mean? No Chinamen are working *here* today or Chinamen aren't working *anywhere* today?"

He gave me a solemn gaze. "This mountain. All mountain. All tunnel. No China man work. Thirty-five dollar good for white man. Forty-five dollar good for China man."

Something was brewing. "How do you know what's going on in all the other tunnels?"

At that his smile broadened. "Make many *zongzi*, bean cake. Hide paper inside. Say: 'Strike on twenty-fifth day.'" He made a sweeping gesture. "Give *zongzi* whole mountain."

Then I remembered the conical packets of food, each tied with red string, that I'd seen coming and going over the past week. I'd figured they were part of some holiday tradition, because the Celestials, it seemed, couldn't go three weeks without commemorating some ancestor or some confluence of stars with specially made food and a ceremony. It was an ongoing waste of time. I'd had no idea the little packets passing back and forth in front of me represented battle plans. "It won't happen," I warned.

"Happen in China. *Zongzi* bring down Kublai Khan."

At that I rolled my eyes. "Apples and oranges. What happened in China doesn't necessarily follow here."

"Must try."

"Why? It's foolishness. They're liable to round you all up and ship you back to China—on separate boats."

Maybe for a second there I saw a shadow of doubt in his eyes, but if that revealed a crack in his resolve, Ducks quickly puttied over it. "Must try," he said firmly. He left off Blind Thomas and crossed his arms. Thomas, of course, sniffed him out to deliver a forceful head butt: *More.*

But Ducks wasn't being dissuaded. "This like tunnel," he said. "Before, no one make tunnel through mountain. Peoples laugh. But China man make this tunnel. How? Look straight. Walk little steps, use hammer, never stop. Just look straight."

I laughed. There he went shoveling out that gibberish of his again; it had to be something peculiar to his people.

"Must teach respect," he continued. And though nothing in the tenor of his voice changed, I got a strong feeling he was speaking directly to me. "No can hammer peoples; no can hammer animals. Hammer for mountain only. Teach respect."

Twenty-One

The gambling fever gripped those mulish Celestials full-time for the next couple of days. They didn't lift a finger to work, but they bet on anything and everything: the number of beans left in the cup, the first magpie to lift off from the cabin roof, the direction a marble would roll. They had no idea they were gambling with their lives—because the railroad came down hard!

Patrick had moved over to my tunnel to lend a temporary hand, but the two of us alone weren't making any progress. So when we heard that some bigwig from the Central Pacific was arriving to make the Celestials toe the mark, we left off our work under the excuse of urgently needing a new set of shafts from the horses' shed. I fastened the feed bag onto Blind Thomas an hour early and tied Brina to the dump cart to keep him company, though she whined her complaint. Then we scurried down to the shed, where we took turns pressing an eyeball to the gap between two slats. There we spied on the gambling game taking place on the other side of the wall, as well as keeping an eye on the path leading up to camp.

It turned out that none other than Charles Crocker himself, one of the Central Pacific Railroad's Big Four, stepped off the supply train that day. Patrick pointed him out to me, though the man was hard to miss, for he must have tipped the scales at well over two hundred pounds. I'd heard of him, of course, because he'd been the one so keen on hiring the Celestials in the first place, even when his partners on the railroad didn't want to. That's why some of the men called them Crocker's Pets. But it wasn't his ample girth that announced his presence so much as his bearing. He came striding up that path with a purpose, the very image of spitting bullets anger. His high forehead and smooth cheeks grew redder and redder with his labored breathing, and I noticed that the row of buttons on his vest bulged to the left and then to the right at each heavy step. Mr. Sikes and Mr. Chang trailed him, along with a couple of other men who looked like railroad potentates. One of them carried a heavy valise. The group marched right up to where one of the gambling games was taking place. Without hesitation Mr. Crocker stepped into its midst and kicked the cup clear across the Celestials' camp.

"Ooh!" Patrick grunted under his breath. "That's what you get for biting the hand that feeds you."

"What do you think he's going to do?" I whispered.

"I don't know, but he's red as a lobster, isn't he? Boiling with wrath, I'd say. Let's see if the pets have any punches."

But it was Mr. Sikes who jumped into the fray next. "Get off your lazy butts," he shouted. "Who's behind this loitering?"

The Chinamen sat as still as stone statues amid the scattered gambling pieces, not acknowledging the loud demand.

"I said, who's behind this?"

That's when Ducks hurried onto the scene, along with three of his cohorts. They spoke to the railroad men in such low voices that I couldn't hear all of what was said. But Mr. Crocker certainly did. "That's ludicrous!" he cried. "Why, I'll shut down this whole operation before I'll give in to those demands!"

"Thirty-five dollar good for white man," Ducks said more loudly, and before he spoke his next words I mouthed them: "Forty-five dollar good for China man."

Mr. Chang stepped in to squawk with his country-men, leaving Mr. Crocker to splutter in anger. He flung his hat to the ground and kicked it. Seemed he was good at kicking things. While Mr. Chang was trying (I assumed) to convince Ducks and the others to give over, Mr. Crocker cast his eye around the camp. His face reddened to a deeper shade. I had to move to the adjoining wall and peer between those boards to find the cause.

Seated beside a stack of empty powder barrels was a cluster of Celestials passing their long pipe. After each took his turn at the mouthpiece, he'd rock back and forth like a windup toy and smile in foggy bliss.

When he realized what was going on, Mr. Crocker's eyes got wide. "Is that what you want more money for," he asked, jerking his ample goatee in their direction, "a bunch of no-good, worthless opium addicts?"

Ducks and his mates exchanged looks that only they could interpret. "No," one of them began, sidling over to block Mr. Crocker's line of sight to the opium party, "money for—"

"Because I'm not forking over my hard-earned dollars so you can stuff it in your pipes," he interrupted. "I *earn* my salary."

"We earn salary. Work hard. Same as white man."

"Doesn't appear to me that a one of you is *working hard*."

More talk was exchanged, but the Celestials' arguments lowered in volume again, so it was difficult to catch all the words. Then Mr. Chang took over, and I couldn't understand the discussion at all. It was when he was speaking though, that I saw a new look settle over Mr. Crocker's features. He began eyeing Mr. Chang and Ducks and even his own man, Mr. Sikes, like he suddenly didn't trust a one of them. Out of nowhere he bellowed, "Is this some sort of chicanery? Are you in collusion with the Union Pacific Railroad? Are they *paying* you to strike?"

All the men, white and Celestial, shook their heads in unison, though some less vigorously than others.

"Of course none of you would admit to it. But it'd be just like that Jack Casement character to fire a cannonball into my business." Mr. Crocker went on musing, voicing his thoughts as he began pacing. It seemed he was searching each face for a weakness or a hint of betrayal. "You all know they get the rights to every mile of land they lay track across, just as we do. So by slowing down the Central Pacific's progress they'd be making money hand over fist." He nodded, buying into his own reasoning. "That's what it is, isn't it? Someone from the U.P. got to one of you"—here he singled out Mr. Chang by stopping in front of him, leaning forward, and nearly touching his huge belly to the man's vest—"lined your pockets with gold to see that all my workers take a holiday?" That encouraged Mr. Sikes to turn his own suspicious eye on the Chinese foreman. Mr. Crocker grabbed the valise from his man, pulled out a money bag, and shook it in the air. The coins inside clinked with tantalizing promises.

Charging again toward the motionless gamblers, he shook the bag over their pigtailed heads. "Well, I'm warning you, you'll not be seeing any more pay from this railroad. And you'll not be getting any more food either. You're not going to use *my* rails to have your extravagant foodstuffs delivered to your doorstep."

"But earn that moneys already," Ducks pleaded. "Family need."

Dang if I didn't know about family need.

Apparently that's what Mr. Crocker was waiting to hear. He whirled like a dust devil. "If your family is depending on you so desperately, then by God, step up. Be a man, and do what it takes to get this money." He shook the bag again, and I saw how his fist strained with the effort, how his thick, sausage fingers blanched with the weight of so much gold.

So much gold.

There stretched a silence then, a stubborn impasse, where everyone's eyes left the money bag and sought haven from Mr. Crocker's stormy face. Except mine. The tension mounted. My heart thudded.

Far in the distance, I heard Brina's bark. It came again, one lone call conveying her worry at being left behind.

"Are you . . . working . . . or are you . . . starving?" The words were meted out like the snaps from a bullwhip. And their threat stung.

"Crap." Patrick pushed away from the shed's wall. "I'm getting back to work before he decides to cut us off, too. You joining me?"

"Yeah, I'm right behind you, but go on ahead."

Patrick grabbed our alibi, the new shafts, and slipped out the door. He took the long way around the shed, away from the battlefront, his feet crunching noisily across the litter of cones and twigs.

So much gold.

I couldn't take my eyes off that bag. The fabric for Ellen's dress was in there, and Sean's boots and a new coat for Ma; the doctor's fee, as well, and food—gobs of food—ham and bread and sugar and tea and cabbage and milk and . . . Mr. Crocker was thrusting the bag at Mr. Sikes now and wagging his finger at Ducks, and I couldn't hear what he was saying, because the blood was pounding in my head. When Mr. Crocker strode away, Mr. Sikes turned to one of the men who had accompanied them. That man juggled the ledger he was carrying and his valise and leaned over to put the money bag inside the valise. While the other men hiked up to the tunnel to inspect the progress, the man with the ledger and the valise hurried toward the train. I shot out the door, commandeered one of the nearby wheelbarrows, and followed. Soon enough we were passing in opposite directions, he hiking back on his return to catch up with his party. I nodded a greeting.

The supplies were being unloaded from the train. There were bags of grain for the horses, and three new pails, and barrel upon barrel of powder, and there, up the steps of the passenger car and mostly hidden inside the door, sat the valise. I glanced around. No one was watching. As smoothly as a practiced criminal I removed the money bag and placed it in the wheelbarrow. Then I loaded the wheelbarrow up with the other supplies, covered it with a tarp, and set off. The air hung so thick around me, it thundered as I pushed the goods and the gold back to the shed.

Twenty-Two

Freshly roasted hare should have had my mouth watering. Especially given that the powerful aroma of it on the green stick was already banishing the memory of the winter's monotonous fare: boiled beef and beans. (Heat and repeat.) But when Jesse, who had bagged the large snowshoe that Sunday morning, proudly served it up on our plates, I found myself barely able to get it down. 'Twas no fault of the hare, though.

Across camp, the Chinaman cook was adding a pail of water to the same soup he'd kept simmering for four days now. No toothsome aromas ascended from that fire.

I shoved the meat around on my plate.

At the start of the strike various tins had been collected into a pile and emptied into the pot, but what was ladled out now looked to be little more than broth. That broth and the ever-present tea were all the Chinamen had to get by on. Mr. Crocker had kept to his word, and not one packet of food traveled by *his* rails to the Chinese strikers.

Forking some meat into my mouth, I tried to look anywhere but there. Yet, again and again my attention swung like a compass needle toward Ducks squatting with his bowl on his knees. He was leading his countrymen with an unflagging appearance of calm. Not one of his actions spoke anger. Even in the composed manner in which he lifted the bowl to his lips and set it down again, he didn't seem overly hungry. Still, when he left off his own thoughts to consider us, the half-lidded gaze he leveled at me weighed heavily.

As if he knew.

"Tasty meat, this," Patrick said loudly, smacking his lips for all to hear. "That was one fat hare."

"Thank you," Jesse replied. "And roasted to perfection if I say so myself."

I glanced away.

The railroad men, I'd heard, were holding Ducks responsible for the missing money bag. Hadn't he been the one, they reasoned, who had claimed the money, saying it had already been earned by him and his fellow workers? Obviously he was the thief. Restitution would be accomplished by withholding his pay for the year to come.

"What's the matter, you don't like my cooking?" Jesse indicated the pile of dark meat still on my plate, fisticuffs in his voice.

I hastily shoved another forkful in my mouth— "Mmm, no! It's delicious. Never tasted finer"—and swallowed with force. "You'll make someone a fine wife," I dared to tease.

Grumbling an oath through his wide grin, Jesse took a swig of coffee and returned to his plate. My eyes swung back to Ducks. Brina had sneaked over to him and was shamelessly resting her nose on his knee, inches from his bowl. The beggar. He scratched her neck.

What happened next made me set down my fork, risking further words from Jesse. Ducks fished around in his bowl and pulled out a sodden morsel of something or other—not much to speak of—but he readily offered it to Brina and smiled when she gulped it down with gratitude. He patted her head.

Inside my belly, the meat settled like rock.

A few days later, Mr. Crocker rode back up the mountain. His railroad associates weren't with him, but a band of well-armed men were. The rifles they carried bristled like the quills of an angry porcupine. With his face flushed hot red, the speech he gave was brief: "I'm putting an end to this nonsense. Today. You'll return to work at the wages offered: $35 a month. No change in your working hours. Those of you who climb off your butts now will be fined for the time lost. Those of you who continue to lounge on the railroad's dime will be fined a month's salary." He passed his blistering glare across the ring of golden faces. "Do I make myself clear?"

To my surprise, several of the Celestials began moving toward the tunnel at once. Ducks squawked. A few of his fellows paused to argue in their own tongue, but it was apparent even to us onlookers that the strike was over. The Celestials walked back to work just as passively as they had walked away from it.

Nothing, seemingly, had changed. Yet in the months to come I discovered that everything had shifted.

Twenty-Three

From the minute I stole that gold, everything that had been pretty much traveling on track for me silently began to tip sideways. With Patrick and Jesse. With Mr. Strobridge. Eventually even with Brina.

We broke through that mountain—*finally!*—in August, meeting up with the other team deep inside the granite bowels to shake hands and exchange echoing hollers of triumph. But when we emerged on the opposite side we were presented with another mountain farther on and challenged to drill another tunnel through it. Where was the victory in that? Ducks was sent to a different crew then, and I no longer saw him, though again and again my thoughts returned to him. Especially when I closed my hands around the heavy pack of mine that concealed the gold he'd been accused of taking.

Without any pay, how was he going to buy his own food from the railroad?

Surely his countrymen would share their food, I argued to myself, trying to ease my guilt. Worthless salve, that.

Winter came and blanketed the mountains once more. But the melting snows in that spring of 1868 found us still inching our way through the Sierra Nevada. Every morning there were more trees to fell, more roots to blast, more rock to drill. A couple of the men on my crew had been breaking their backs on this "great enterprise" for more than four and a half years now, yet we figured that in all that time only about a hundred miles of rail had been laid. At an unimaginable cost, too, I was certain. Rumors swirled among us that during those same years, our rival—the Union Pacific Railroad, which was laying track westward from Omaha—had covered six times that much territory.

"Nebraska's flat as a pancake," Jesse grumbled in retort. "Anybody's grandma can lay track across flat land." Still, it stung to labor on the losing team.

When I was beginning to believe that I'd spend the rest of my life as a blinking mole inside a tunnel, we poked clear through to the eastern side of the Sierra Nevada, inched our way down its slopes, and joined the men who had already begun constructing a grade across the desert. I got a good understanding then of how the rail work organized by the Central Pacific stretched more than a hundred miles in both directions. Based on weather and terrain, there was always some phase of blasting, clearing, and grading taking place somewhere along the proposed line. Trestles across gorges or rivers were built well ahead of the rails. Newly dug quarries stood ready to supply ballast. And once the tracks arrived, towns sprang up overnight. In building the grade, we'd come across a little mud-brick home with a man and woman and a couple of pigs, then, happening by a week later, discovered that with the arrival of the rails there was now a saloon and a lodging establishment and even a respectable mercantile. It was a wonder.

In the course of those many months my life continued taking a turn. I went from tunneling to grading, from shivering to sweating, from boy to, well, man. Because by the summer of 1868 I'd actually outstripped Jesse. And though Patrick still edged me by a hair, my shoulders were broader than his. So some of my pay began going toward the purchase of clothes. I was busting out of shirt seams before the fabric even got comfortable. I'd grown that much.

The rest of my pay I sent right home, of course, eighty-some dollars in that first mailing, after repaying

Jesse close to a hundred. ("A pleasure doing business with you," he said cockily, and that made me want to deal the cards then and there to win my money back.) I'd sent Ma her scarf, along with some licorice candies for Margaret and Sean and little Ellen, and an Indian arrowhead that Jesse said he'd pulled out of his own leg after being chased by some Apache in Arizona Territory. That cost me another fifty cents. After that, though, almost everything that I had left over from my card playing and my clothes buying was regularly mailed home.

But for some reason I couldn't part with the stolen gold. Each time that we'd crossed a town with a post office—Truckee in California, Reno and Wadsworth in Nevada—places where I had the opportunity to trade it in for a postal money order and send it to my family in New York, I couldn't bring myself to do it.

Why? The money gave me no pleasure. I'd secretly wrapped the troublesome coins in paper to keep them from announcing themselves, then stuffed the heavy packets back inside the railroad's money bag and then buried the whole lot inside an old shirt at the bottom of my haversack. No one knew it was there except me. And maybe Ducks.

Thinking back, I saw how I'd grabbed it in haste; I was that desperate to answer Ma's pleas, and panicked, too, about my rising gambling losses. So why hadn't I used the coins to satisfy either of those problems? Keeping them hidden, having to glance constantly toward that dark corner under my bunk, was more than wearisome. It was a day-to-day burden that I longed to confess and unload. But I couldn't. What would Patrick and Jesse say? What would the railroad do? I honestly didn't know how to get myself out of this mess. And so it rubbed at me every day, like a stone in my boot, working its way through my flesh.

After the hot, dry days, summer evenings were enjoyably cool in the desert, and Brina and I often sat watching the stars turn in the sky. I regularly sought out Cowboy and Weaver Girl, Ducks's lovelorn stars separated by the Milky Way, though I couldn't tell if they were moving closer. Nor could I decipher if any of the sparse rains that teased the barren land fell especially healing, though I'd gladly have paid for some of that special water to ease my sore stomach.

In gazing up at the glittery sky, I thought how it presented a vast storybook to Ducks, one sprinkled with poignant tales, heroic characters, and long-departed loved ones. It was a guidebook to life that he could reference at any time. But to me? To me those same stars swirled dizzily above my head, revealing nothing and pointing me nowhere. I felt fairly certain that even Cowboy and Weaver Girl looked down upon me and shook their heads, leaving me to wander on my own.

Twenty-Four

"Jesus!" Patrick cried, kicking and dancing with a fury. A scorpion sailed past me, hit a nearby rock with the faint *scritch* of a dried leaf, and, having slid to the desert floor, clambered on its way in no more hurry than before.

"Aw, you found another pet," Jesse teased. His chuckle caught in his throat, and he spent some time clearing it before continuing. "Must be your sweet temper that draws the little critters to ya."

Patrick shuddered and shook his head. "I can't abide anything with more than four legs—or less than two. Give me snow and cold and eight months of winter in the mountains, but keep your dang desert scorpions and snakes and such to yourself." Retrieving his shovel, he stabbed the hard-baked ground. The blade made only a faint imprint. He scanned the horizon and shook his head again. "What a godforsaken land."

"Well, let's get on with it," Jesse said. "Must be only another hundred miles or so to the end of this hell." He dug his shovel into the grade we were building, and the effort set him to coughing again. It was that chesty, raggedy sort that presses a knife to your own throat and makes you swallow hard. Spittle dappled his shirtfront, and when he wiped his sleeve across his nose, the fabric came away streaked with red.

An echoing cough sounded on the opposite side of the grade and, farther back, another one. It was only morning, sometime in the fall of 1868, and the desert sky was still a pearly gray. But the air was thin and dry, and the invisible breath of the desert exhaled the promise of unseasonable heat. The dust that would kick up—pure alkali—would soon cake us in white. Hat brims, shoulders, fingernails, belt buckles—all would be rimed with white before time was called. Noses and mouths and lungs would suck in the stuff; the alkali would burn holes through tissue and send blood spurting out noses and sometimes mouths.

The railroad was pushing us—all of us, man as well as animal—brutally. For months now we'd been tramping across this Nevada wasteland. Track was being laid at three to four miles a day, an impressive pace to my way of thinking. But not to the kingfish. They wanted more, always more. Earlier, at the height of the season's heat, one of the railroad bigwigs had seen fit to wire these encouraging words: "So work on as though Heaven was before you and Hell behind you."

He must have been speaking from the velvet cushion of his almighty throne, probably having to set aside his cigar to send those words of wisdom. Like hell was behind us? We lived in hell. We camped in hell, walked over hell, slept, ate, and crapped in hell. The sun—on its fieriest days—seared our skin like the Devil himself was stubbing out his cigar on us. It burned right through our clothes, even. And the dust of that great sinkhole—a fine, acrid powder—got in our lungs to burn through from the other side. That's what accounted for all the coughing.

Water was the answer, but the farther we got into the desert, the farther we got from the liquid relief. Some days, it had to be hauled in wooden barrels as much as thirty or forty miles, and by the time it arrived it tasted hot and a little brackish. Then, even though our tongues were swollen and sticky with our own breathing, we had to force ourselves to swallow it.

That barrel water sloshed around your gut like it was inside a cave, and you could smell the stagnant air in your nose and taste the slime on the back of your throat. It didn't even cool you; rather, it seemed to evaporate right through your pores, leaving a salty skim you could flick off with your fingernail. It was like one of those desert mirages: you saw the water, and you felt it going down your throat, but never once did you stop being thirsty and never did you have to take a whiz. The stuff simply disappeared, like every drop of water that chanced to fall on this stingy desert. The land was so dry, the joke was that even the jackrabbits shouldered canteens. Brina herself had given up following me out to the work site and spent her days panting beneath the shade of the meal car.

Yes, day-to-day living here whittled you down to the bone, thin and hard. The work either broke you or honed you.

I let it hone me. I actually sort of liked this harsh land. It demanded grit to survive in it, and when I looked around, I saw that only a few plants and animals succeeded at it. I was going to be one of them. The desert—along with the railroad bosses—were throwing calculated punches, but I was punching back.

"Hey!" One of the men working farther along the grade called to us. "Come take a look at this."

Jesse and Patrick and I exchanged glances, shouldered our picks and shovels, and hiked ahead. Curious, other workers followed, and for a moment there in the desert, the building of the Central Pacific Railroad came to a halt.

As a group we encircled a tall, weathered cross

pole bearing the plainly lettered name LUCINDA DUNCAN. A few small boulders had been arranged at the base of the pole, to protect the grave from wandering wolves, I suppose, and these were dusted with windblown grit and seed hulls. Obviously poor Lucinda had spent many a year out here alone in the desert.

"What do you suppose happened to her?" a man named Eli said, removing his hat.

"Probably traveling with her family on one of them wagon trains," another replied. He, too, removed his hat, prompting the rest of us to pay our respects. "Probably got sick and died."

"Or killed by Indians."

"Or bit by a scorpion," said Patrick.

"Nah, scorpion won't kill you," Eli said.

"How do you know? You been bit by one?"

"No, but I know. They won't kill you. Just make you sick."

"So maybe a scorpion bit her and she got sick and then she died."

Eli considered that. "Maybe. I'll bet she was a pretty thing, though. Pretty name: Lucinda."

"How come they didn't put any dates on it?" I asked, nodding up at the pole. "We don't know how long she's been dead or even how old she was." For some reason, that really bothered me.

"I put her at fifteen," Eli said with authority, "or maybe sixteen. Lucinda sounds like a girl about fifteen. With golden hair gathered into a ribbon." He stared at the bleak grave with such a long face that it might have been his own sister. "Hope she didn't have to suffer."

Silence.

One of the workers measured the sight line to the eastern horizon. "The way the railroad's got this staked, the tracks are going to run right through here. I don't cotton to the idea of poor Lucinda being rattled by locomotives day and night."

Our bowed heads shook in unison.

Jesse looked over his shoulder. "Boss won't be out this way for a while. If we all join in the digging, shouldn't take too much of the railroad's time to relocate her." He pointed to higher ground a short distance away. "That little hill would do; it's got a nice view of the valley. Patrick, Malachy, you take some others and start digging a new grave up there. We'll dig here."

Spurred on by purpose, we divided into two teams and in under an hour poor stiff Lucinda, wrapped in her sheet, was reburied a peaceful distance south of the railway with a nice view of the wide valley. The old cross pole traveled with her. And a pile of rocks protected the freshly turned soil.

"She needs a proper headstone," Eli said, frowning.

"Where are we going to get a headstone? Besides, there's no time for that."

"And a little white fence would be nice. So people know it's a graveyard."

"It's not a graveyard," argued Patrick gently, "it's one grave."

"It's Lucinda's graveyard."

More silence followed, and I became aware of the number of Celestials who'd gathered. Without our asking it, they'd quietly joined in the reburial, scouring the desert for rock and lugging it in wheelbarrows back to the new gravesite. I suspected they questioned why Lucinda's family would abandon her to the desert—though nothing showed on their faces—because I'd seen how stubborn they were about returning their own dead to San Francisco, or even all the way to China, to rejoin family. Honoring the dead seemed to be of high importance to them. Ducks had certainly burned enough strips of paper and set out enough rice bowls over the seasons, remembering his eight friends killed in the snow slide as well as his own ancestors. But whatever their criticism of our burial practices, the Celestials said nothing.

As we headed back to the grading I turned to have a last look at the pole jutting from the hill. It gave me a churchy feeling—the hill, the cross, the great expanse of blue sky stretching up to the heavens—and I got filled up with the good deed we'd done. Lucinda could rest easy now, watching the trains go by; maybe they'd even sound their whistles for her.

I felt lighter too. Exactly one gold coin lighter, because I'd slipped one into the shovelful of dirt I was adding to her grave. That made about as much sense as Ducks burning his paper money because, really, how could the dead spend it? I suppose I was doing it for me, trying to unburden myself in some small way.

We worked the rest of the morning in relative silence, lost in our own thoughts (and I'm guessing here) of life and death and far-off family. Then, when the sun peaked in the sky, we set down our picks and shovels and hiked back for a break. Brina always crawled out from under the meal car to greet me, stretching her limbs and grinning sheepishly. Or maybe she crawled out to beg scraps from dinner plates; food had always been high on her list of priorities. The horses took their break, too, and back by the feed car I noticed Blind Thomas standing alone and swinging his head back and forth like a pendulum. He was fretting, as was his nature.

Obviously the kid working him had gone off for his own meal without watering the poor horse or strapping on the noon feed bag. Feeling my neck grow hot—and *not* because of the sun—I hurried over.

"Easy, there, Thomas," I said, announcing my

presence. He didn't seem to hear me, because he kept to his swaying. "Thomas," I said again, and one ear swiveled in my direction. I saw then that his bridle had been fastened too tight, drawing his lips back in an unnatural grimace. Laying a hand on his sweaty neck and working my way up to his head, I managed to loosen the buckles. Then I ran my fingers beneath the bridle straps, rubbing at the sticky patches, and scratched the tips of his scabby ears where the biting insects tormented him. Eventually he started to relax. Since the lazybones kid was nowhere in sight, I took the responsibility of leading Thomas over to the watering barrel.

He smelled it before we got there, of course, and began stretching his neck, blindly testing for the water's surface. His busy lips wriggled in anticipation. When he made contact with the water, he splashed playfully at first, soaking the ground and my boots, before drinking deeply. His long throat muscles expanded and contracted like a glistening black snake. When he was finished drinking— and this was his habit—he plunged his head deep into the barrel all the way to his ears and swished it around with animal glee. I'd never in my life seen a horse enjoy water the way he did, and I laughed out loud.

"I was gonna do that, you know." The good-for-nothing kid stood with his hands in his pockets, his fat lower lip bunched in a pout. Bean sauce mottled his chin.

"Save your 'gonnas,'" I retorted. "He's thirsty now." Then, giving him my best glare, I said, "He works a sight harder than you. You should see to his needs first."

The lip puckered and pushed forward, further distorting the mumbled words: "He's just a horse."

Thomas tossed his head, showering me with water that did nothing to cool my ire. "What? What did you say?"

For a moment I thought he was going to back away, but the kid surprised me by shoving his hands deeper into his pockets and blaring an accusation. "He's just a horse, and he's a loony one at that. We're supposed to change out horses midday, but he won't have it. Soon as I tie him to the car, he bucks and pulls back till his halter breaks. Then he comes trotting to the fore and getting all the other horses lathered. Doesn't have the sense to enjoy a rest when he's given it."

"That's because he knows his work and takes pride in it. He's not some sort of lie-abed slug, like you."

The kid recoiled, though not out of fear, because I'd seen that same cold-eyed consideration in a rattlesnake I'd happened to disturb—and managed to sidestep—a few months back. He delivered his words with deliberate venom: "Is he a thief, like you?"

I threw a punch but was so off balance in holding on to Thomas that the kid was able to duck out of the way, smirking. Letting go of the reins, I started after him.

"Here now!" One of the foremen was suddenly pushing his horse between us. "Break it up! Get back to your work, both of you. And mind that loose horse."

The kid scrambled for safety and made a show of fussing over Blind Thomas's harness. My palms itched to lay him flat. A quaking sea of red and yellow jumbled my vision.

"I said, *get back to your work!*"

Forced away from any such satisfaction, I stalked back up the rails without stopping for anything to eat. I stalked all the way to where we'd been hacking at a rocky outcropping, mining the gravel and sand to build up the grade.

How did he know? I grabbed a pick and took a swing at the exposed rock. The jarring connection, a shock to my wrists and arms and shoulders, felt nearly as good as a punch. What did he know exactly? And who else knew? A large chunk began to loosen. I hit it again. Then I wedged the pick behind it and tugged. It wobbled. I tugged harder, repositioned the pick once more, and set all my weight against it, but I couldn't get the right leverage. Dropping the pick and grabbing the loosened rock with both hands, I heaved backward. I felt the strain in my legs and my back. And a sharp, burning sting on my hand. From the corner of my eye I saw the pincher claws and wickedly curled tail of a scorpion as it scuttled back into the shadows.

I let go of the rock to stumble backward, surprised and scared. At once an ominous tingling began traveling up my arm, like fire ants crawling through my veins. My throat tightened; I felt like I couldn't breathe. And then I really couldn't breathe.

Help. I know I mouthed the word, but nothing came out. Blinking, trying to hold on to consciousness, I felt a giant dizziness swamping me. In slow motion I crumpled to the ground, gasping for air like poor, dying Lucinda.

Twenty-Five

Eli was right: You don't die from a scorpion's sting, but for a while you wish you would. I lay on the ground for I don't know how long, struggling just to breathe. A terrifying numbness wormed its way through my body; it crept past my wrist and up to my armpit, then across my chest, and with invisible fingers set a choke hold around my neck. I knew I had to stay calm, so I closed my eyes and counted deliberate breaths of air.

But confusion fogged my thinking. I couldn't keep track of the numbers—thirty-seven? seventy-four?—and I couldn't remember where I was or what I was supposed to be doing. A roaring filled my ears. Gravel poked my face. In my delirium I sensed some poisonous sheet wrapping around me in preparation for burial.

Then, through the haze, came angel voices accompanied by rough hands. A bumpy ride in a wheelbarrow delivered me to a shaded cot where wet cloths were pressed to my chest and face. "Good Lord," one of them exclaimed, "will you look at the size of his arm?" And it was lifted into the air for holy examination: a thief's arm, in all its bloated glory.

Fitful dreams and fragmented sentences rushed across me as summer storms over the desert. Time must have rolled on too, because when light next tickled my eyelids I found myself in the doctor's car among a number of other bedridden casualties. My body felt strangely numb and at the same time allover tingly. My lips, my toes, even the tips of my ears, felt numb. As I lay there blinking and trying to come to my senses, though, I did feel something: a wet pressure on my fingers. Shifting my gaze sideways, I found Brina earnestly licking my hand. When she noticed I was awake, she wriggled up to my shoulder and plunked her blocky head right next to it, shoving hard with her nose. Her honey eyes sparked, and her tail wagged so enthusiastically that her back end performed a solo waltz. "Hey, lass," I said, and lifted my good hand to pat her head.

Footsteps approached and a voice, a baritone, rose in mild protest: "Here now! Out with you!" His clapping sent Brina darting for the door, and in her place a tall man with a pink complexion bent over to enter my view. He had fine, polished hands, those of a gentleman, and he laid the cool tips of his fingers on my forehead. "How are you feeling, son?"

"I'm okay," I replied, surprised at how the words climbing out of my dry throat croaked and caught on one another.

He pulled up a stool, took out a pen, and consulted his clipboard. "What did you tangle with out there—snake, scorpion?"

"Scorpion. 'Twas a little one, though."

He frowned and nodded, digesting the information. Then, leaning in with a shy smile, he said, "It's always the little ones that pack the biggest wallop, isn't it?" I tried to nod back, but he was already about his examination, a trace of his smile lingering as he gently probed my arm and chest and neck. Humming to himself, he spun away to produce a medicine bottle and pour out a spoonful. "Here, this will help with the pain," he said, and before I knew it, the sticky stuff was past my lips and coating my scratchy throat. He patted my leg, finished. "Time's the best healer in your case," he said. "You make that cot your home for a while."

The tall doctor visited the other cots in the car one by one, dispensing spoonfuls of medicine and adjusting bandages, then returned to his stool. "I've just this morning come into possession of a newspaper from Salt Lake City. A family traveling west in their wagon handed it to me. Would any of you care to hear the happenings, though they be dusty and dated?"

Of course we did and, to a one, I think, turned our faces toward him like expectant children awaiting a story.

"Let's see, let's see. What can I find of interest to you? Hmm, there's been a fight at a saloon in Corrine."

"Not likely that that's news!"

Ignoring the commentary, he read aloud. "It says here that a man by the name of Wild Jack sliced the wrist of a stranger because he thought he'd been insulted. 'A fight ensued in which Wild Jack crawled through a window and escaped.'" The doctor pursed his lips and shook his head. "What's the matter with people nowadays? Is there to be no common decency?" His chin rose and fell as he continued perusing the narrow columns of type. "How about this? 'A lady named Bloundell, sixty-three years of age, fell into a cellar near Brigham City, on Friday last, and . . . received injuries that will probably prove fatal.' Oh, that's too bad." He shook his head again. "But here now: 'On July 7, to the wife of J. S. Barrie, was born a daughter, Josephine.' See? Life balances out."

"What about the railroad?" someone asked. "What's the news? How far has the U.P. come?"

The dried paper crackled between the doctor's fingers as he scanned its pages. "Railroad . . . railroad. Oh, here! 'On Wednesday morning last a brakeman named Albert Sussman, while attempting to couple cars about eight miles east of Ogden . . .'" His voice slowed as it trailed off. "'. . . had his right hand crushed. He was treated by Dr. S. P. Thomas'—now, there's the good in it; he's a fine physician: I can personally attest to that—'and taken to Salt Lake City for further attention.'"

It seemed the newspaper was full of mishaps and tragedies; appropriate, I suppose, for a car filled with the sick and wounded. But whether it included any real railroad news was lost to me because the doctor's words became garbled in my ears as a drowsiness took hold of my body. My eyelids grew heavy, and I slept.

When I woke again, Patrick and Jesse were clambering noisily into the car. I didn't know how much time had passed. Recognizing one of the others, Patrick gave a nod and said, "Hello there, Francis. How's the knee?"

"On the mend, on the mend. Itchy for a little poker, though. You and the others got a game going this Saturday?"

Patrick flashed a grin. "I'll get my stout friend here to carry you over to the table himself," he said, clapping Jesse on the shoulder.

Jesse lifted his eyebrows and delivered a skeptical look to both of them before turning to me. "Well, you're looking a mite better. Yesterday you were popping sweat and pale as a sheet, all the while moaning like you were possessed. Seemed you had some big secret to tell, but there wasn't a one of us could understand it."

I panicked a bit at that.

"Jesus! Your fingers look like sausages," Patrick said.

"Nah, his are bigger than what they dished up at breakfast."

"Those weren't sausages, I'm telling you. But I'll not be the one asking Cookie about it."

Their mutual laugh ignited a smile on my face.

"Hey," Patrick said, "we've graded well past Lucinda now, and the boss didn't say anything about us moving her gravesite. Don't think he even noticed."

"That Eli character's still set on building a white picket fence for her, though. Heard he was scrounging around for lumber scraps."

"So how are you feeling? You need anything?"

I was worried about the gold coins, of course, but I couldn't come right out and ask about them.

"We're looking after your things," Jesse said.

My heart quickened, but I was pretty sure I could trust these two.

"Indeed," Patrick added. "I lashed your haversack to mine for safekeeping. Heavy enough. You packing iron horse shoes or something?"

Feeling sort of dopey and drowsy again, I said, "Yeah, I'm gathering good luck."

We talked some more, I think, or they talked and I listened; but I was still having a great deal of trouble staying awake, so perhaps I drifted off on them, because when I next awoke they were gone.

At supper, bowls of beef and beans were delivered to those of us in the doctor's car, but I had to leave my spoon standing in the stew. I couldn't taste it, couldn't taste anything. Was this all because of the scorpion sting? What had happened to me?

Brina snuck back into the car to gently lick my swollen hand while wriggling in excitement. I rubbed her silky ears. 'Twas good to have such a faithful friend, one who stood beside you, wagging, no matter what you did.

Twenty-Six

It took more than a couple of weeks to shake off that scorpion sting. I came down with a fever soon afterward, which led to a rash that oozed pus and wouldn't heal. Then lice got into my clothes and hair and skin. Mother of God! Minus the locusts descending on camp, it was like I was suffering the plagues of old Egypt.

But the outside of me eventually healed, and I was put on a crew quarrying rock to ballast the railroad ties and tracks. As another winter approached, brisk winds rushed across the land to fling grit against our faces, and I, for one, actually began to miss the protection of the mountain tunnels. An official postmaster arrived on one of the supply trains to deliver mail and gather letters and parcels and postal money orders in advance of Christmas. Ma's letter this time reported that Ellen was now sick, Sean needed a new shirt for his confirmation, and the rent was overdue. And she had no money to buy her children presents. I handed over all my pay to the postmaster and even managed to dig a few more coins, unseen, from the stolen gold and send that amount as well. Still, it didn't seem enough.

We couldn't locate a tree to erect that Christmas—the desert was too barren—and the day passed absent any cheer. Some of the men borrowed horses and rode off in search of entertainment. I chose to stay behind. For a while, Brina and I paged through a dime novel about an Indian and his pet wolf, but the words came hard to me and, growing frustrated, I set it aside. Finally got out my cards (I had my own deck now) and spent the time practicing my shuffling and dealing.

A week later it was 1869, and tensions seemed to be building because the two competing railroad companies were closing in on each other. Reports came in that the advancing grades were actually running parallel to each other, with each company—the Central Pacific and the Union Pacific—hoping to get rails laid first and thus claim the land.

Come March, I was back in the doctor's car. Not because I was injured but because Jesse had ridden out looking for entertainment and found some—in the form of a bullet lodged in his shoulder. He claimed he'd been minding his own business and been fired upon for no good reason. None of us questioned his story to his face, of course, but we painted many different—and more likely—scenarios while he was laid up.

In visiting him I found the same doctor reading aloud from a newspaper. He looked up as I entered and paused midsentence. "Hello, there! You get yourself stung again?"

"No. Just came by to visit my hotheaded friend." And I pointed to Jesse.

"It wasn't my fault!" he protested. "I didn't do nothing, I'm telling you!" A white bandage with a coin-size circle of blood seeping through it wrapped his exposed shoulder. His hair was matted to his forehead, and he looked sort of beaten down.

Taking just a wee bit of pleasure in his misery, I said, "Shh! It's story hour," and motioned for the doctor to continue.

"'. . . said woman cracked an egg over her husband's head and let his two dogs do the bathing.'"

A man in a cot against the opposite wall rose onto his elbows to ask, "Doctor, what does it say about the railroads? Have they decided yet where they're going to join up?"

"Well, let's see." The doctor turned the page. "Here's a report on the construction." He scanned the column, reading aloud the most provocative sentences. "'Work is being vigorously prosecuted. . . . Grading camps present the appearance of a mighty army with tents, wagons, and men as far as the eye can see. . . . Both lines running near each other and occasionally crossing.'" That gave him pause, and he looked up. "Is this true? The Union Pacific is building their grade *across* ours?"

"Not only across our grade," said the man hoisted onto his elbows, "but stealing the fill dirt from it. Went out one morning last week and found those U.P. scalawags had dug four feet of dirt from our grade to add to theirs."

"Bunch of no-account thieves, they are," added another.

"What do you and your men do in such a situation?"

The man on his elbows looked surprised, as if the answer were all too obvious. "Why, we stole it right back, of course. It's our dirt. Shoveled it into our own wheel-barrows and returned it to our grade. That's where it belongs."

The doctor nodded in his thoughtful manner. "Mm-hmm. All right." And returned to the newspaper. "Let's see. . . . 'Blasters are jarring the earth every few minutes with—'"

As if on cue, a not-too-distant explosion rattled the car. Glass bottles clinked, and the shimmery air sent dust motes dancing.

"'—their glycerine and powder, lifting whole ledges

of limestone rock from their long resting places, hurling them hundreds of feet in the air and scattering them around for a half mile in every direction.' I must say," he commented, "this reporter certainly has captured the scene." The car remained silent as he searched for more tidbits. "Oh, here it says there was a blasting accident out near Carmichael's Cut. 'After pouring in the powder they undertook to work it down with iron bars. The bars striking the rocks caused an explosion, and one of the men was blown two hundred feet in the air—'"

That elicited a low whistle from his listeners.

"'—breaking every bone in his body; the other three men were terribly burnt and wounded with flying stones.'"

"I heard about that one," Jesse told me. A second explosion, and then another hard upon it, like answering cannon fire, rained pebbles on the roof.

From a cot in the far corner came a muffled wail. "Oh, now, haven't I had too much of that in the war to ever grow accustomed to it."

"Welcome to the new war, then," his neighbor replied, "because the U.P. is, in essence, attacking us. They're lighting their fuses without first notifying our crews. That's what happened to me." He pointed to his leg, bandaged ankle to thigh and set in a brace.

The newspaper was lowered as attention shifted to him.

"You all know how far we've been grading ahead of the rails. It's going to be a big loss for one company—and I pray it's the U.P.—but the thing is, it's getting more and more dangerous with this side-by-side blasting. One minute you're minding your own business, and the next—*boom!*— you're airborne along with a wagonload of flying rock. I came down with only a busted leg but another, Johnny Asher—some of you know him—got sent back to the city still unconscious. A bunch of the Celestials on our crew got banged up pretty bad too; big rock came loose and rolled over 'em, knocked 'em down like bowling pins. One of the blasts even killed two of our mules right where they stood."

"Well, better mules than men," the doctor said.

"Better than Irish men, you mean," growled a voice I hadn't heard before. "Those pigtailed foreigners aren't really men."

I found myself cringing at that. Despite Ducks's quacking and caterwauling, his peculiar ceremonies and all that bathing, he'd proven himself a man on more than one occasion. Wherever he was now, I wished him well.

"But they're fine workers," the doctor countered. He folded the newspaper and crossed his legs. "I've heard it commented many a time that these Chinese are quick learners and nearly equal to white men once trained in the work they are to perform. Mr. Crocker himself has said the very same."

"Aye, and wouldn't he be the one to go bragging on his little pets."

"Saying it's so doesn't make it so," protested the man with the busted leg. "And I don't think they work that hard. I've never seen a one of them in any kind of a hurry, except when they're heading off for their tea breaks, which is practically every fifteen minutes."

I did have to agree with that.

"The thing is, there's just so danged many of them." The speaker surveyed the room for agreement. "If they weren't here, we'd get paid a whole lot more, you know. And we wouldn't have to work near as hard, either. I think maybe someone should run them out of the country."

"Amen to that."

"The U.P.'s doing fine without the Chinese," someone added.

"And quick to tell us about it. 'We're the Union Pacific,'" came a man's mocking voice, "'and we've laid a thousand miles of track. We're the Union Pacific, and we can lay eight miles of track in a day.'"

"Aw, anybody's grandmother can lay track across flat land," Jesse broke in. "I'd like to see how they'd fare in the peaks of the Sierra Nevada."

A new voice spoke. "Aw, don't go believing all their

supposed records. I have it on good authority that the U.P.'s measuring sticks are mighty rubbery."

The conversation got animated then, and the doctor set aside his newspaper to listen. Jesse's eyes sparked, which told me he wasn't hurting too bad. "There's a wager in here somewhere," he said. "I've just got to figure out who's holding the money."

Twenty-Seven

Clear, cold moonlight streamed across my twisted blanket, washing it of color. Since I wasn't getting any sleep—as was usual, now—I crept outside our car to have a ramble. Brina shook herself awake, yawned, and willingly followed at my side, halting now and then to cock an ear at the muffled sounds peculiar to our sleeping camp.

This wasn't our first "wee hours of the morning" walk. My feet, through their own restlessness, had taken to twitching and kicking at slumber. So I'd begun using them to explore the outskirts of our ever-advancing campsite.

We'd crossed into Utah Territory in early April, and the moonlit salt flats shimmered like polished silver. An enormous lake lapped at us from the south, its mirrored surface stretching all the way to the horizon. From its waters, just a little way out, rose a solitary, pyramid-shaped rock that seemed to serve as Nature's sentinel to the momentous happenings on shore. Nothing like this had ever been seen.

Just inland from the shoreline sprawled a huge Chinese camp with what I counted as close to three hundred tents. I knew Mr. Crocker was marshaling his crews for the final push to the finish, but the numbers were jaw dropping. Curious, I let my feet carry me in that direction and stood on the hillside looking down at them.

An icy breeze off the lake fingered a few tent flaps (and nipped my nose), but other than that a tranquil air enveloped the camp. Standing there in the dark reminded me of the time I'd watched Ducks fly his kite with the little lanterns. That ceremonial good-bye had stirred something inside me, and I'd often brought it to mind since for the warmth it gave. I wondered if the eight bodies had been recovered after the spring thaw. Their abandonment troubled me, and I hoped someone had at least made the effort. I wondered, too, as I often did, what had happened to Ducks. In the shadows of my mind his cat eyes still followed me everywhere. Is that why I couldn't sleep?

Brina sighed and sat. I sank to the ground as well and hugged her to me. She was too busy listening to the sounds privy only to dogs to return the affection. Her head turned from side to side like a weathervane as she deciphered the night. Employing my limited senses, I caught the soft voice of a night bird winging overhead and the faint splash of a creature in the lake; other than that, hers was a world locked to me.

After some time, a distant tent flap opened and a small, dark-clothed Celestial emerged. He moved through the gloom to a private spot behind his tent to relieve himself, then hurried, hunched against the cold, to stir his cooking fire. Orange embers sprang to life. Another tent flap lifted, and the predawn ritual repeated. Then another and another. As the camp of the Celestials awakened, Brina collapsed across my lap and dozed. My sleepless eyelids remained propped wide open. Like a windblown wildfire, the orange sparks multiplied throughout the camp, blossoming into flames that boiled tea and sizzled meats and greens.

Another day's work was about to begin, and I was looking forward to it. The meeting place for the two railroads had finally been set: Promontory Summit. For bragging rights, each wanted to get there first, and so construction proceeded at a frenzied pace. Stoking the competitive fires, the Union Pacific sent regular reports of how many miles of track they'd laid that day, never missing an opportunity to remind us of their momentous eight-miles-in-a-day record. Some of the men, including me, wanted to try to equal it, but the foremen responded with a united warning to bide our time.

Breathing in a lungful of the crisp desert air, I released it with a sigh.

Stars began to wink out, and the activity in the graying light below me increased. Orderly lines formed for the food and tea being served. Of course, with the Celestials, there was none of the elbowing that plagued our meal lines.

Having lifted Brina's head from my lap, I was just climbing to my feet when a group of Chinamen in high spirits approached their cook. What was the cause of their tomfoolery? Had they been drinking all night, or smoking their pipes? A staccato laugh traveled up the hillside, chased by another. Something, obviously, was really funny. Then here came the individual provoking their amusement. Taller than the rest, he walked with measured steps and an outstretched arm. Something balanced on his palm and, through the murkiness of the dawn, I was pretty sure I identified the slender silhouette of a pick. My chest got tight. I squinted hard, trying to make sure. But there was no doubt. It was Ducks.

Twenty-Eight

We soon discovered that Mr. Crocker was just as eager as we were to best the Union Pacific, but he'd been cleverly calculating the ideal opportunity. He waited until the very end of April, when the Central Pacific's railhead was sixteen miles west of Promontory Summit and the U.P.'s was only nine miles to the east of it, then announced that C.P. men could lay *ten* miles of workable track in a day.

The U.P. officials must have laughed outright. Such a claim was ludicrous. But bets were placed, and the date for the record-setting attempt was set: April 28, 1869. And we were put to the test.

When I sat on the metal steps of the car, that still-dark morning, the ground seemed to vibrate. It felt like a rumbling of distant forces, of the earth, having awakened from her slumber to discover too late our battle plans, hastily summoning her own armies: her magnifying sun, her cold wind, her bone-rattling rock. Such hubris! Mere humans couldn't nail ten miles of track to her desert floor in one day. We must be stopped. We *would* be stopped.

Back inside the car, Patrick bolted upright in his bunk and reached for his boots. "They sound the whistle yet?"

I shook my head and bent to lace my own boots, a nervous smile creasing my lips. This was *our* day at last. When Mr. Crocker and Mr. Strobridge and the others had set their sights on laying ten miles in a day, they'd bet their money on us: the Irish. And we were determined to deliver.

Brina rose to her feet, tail wagging. The predawn gloom fairly crackled with expectation, and the hairs on my forearms lifted. In reaching for my gloves I found my hands already so warmed, the blood pulsing right down to my fingertips, that I stuffed the unnecessary gear into my pocket instead. A tremor of excitement infiltrated our sleeping car unseen, nudging the others awake one by one and, when they realized the day, sending them scrambling for coats and hats and out the door. Encouraging nods were exchanged. Winks dispersed. Grinning ever wider, I hurried shoulder-to-shoulder with them. Brina, nose in the air, trotted happily at our side.

All along the railway, men milled beneath the fading

stars, chatting briskly while making preparations. Horses were hitched to wagons or fitted with saddles, spikes were counted and recounted; muscles were unknotted, necks stretched loose.

The cooking fires that glowed throughout the Chinese camps turned the endless white tents into a thousand resting moths. Shadowy figures moved among the tents, also making preparations. Over and over I'd heard how they—or their ancestors, at least—had built some great wall in China. Apparently that was quite a feat. But today was the day when the sons of Eire would accomplish a feat the world had never seen.

Eight Irishmen had been chosen to begin laying rail, and they were Edward Killeen, George Elliott, Michael Kennedy, and Michael Sullivan; then Thomas Daley, Fred McNamara, another Michael, surname Shay, and my very own mate, Patrick Joyce.

Another eight were named to the relief crew, ordered to stand at the ready, because no human could continually lift quarter-ton rails, one after another, for a whole ten miles.

The name Malachy Gormley wasn't called.

Maybe I shouldn't have expected to be chosen, what with those weeks I'd spent in the doctor's car. But I wanted the chance to prove myself. I have to admit I took off after the selection, storming past the blacksmith's car, my fists clenching and unclenching, and on past the harness shop and the sleeping quarters, and finally pacing hot circles near the feed car. All things being considered, didn't I measure up to the best of them? For the past two years I'd worked alongside Patrick and the others as an equal, swinging the same sledge and hauling the same rock. I was as tall as any and as broad as most. Younger, yes, but just as strong. Oh, how I wanted to be one of those eight! But Mr. Strobridge, having consulted with our foreman, called Patrick's name to the list of eight and not mine, and the bag of barley I hung from a nail on the side of the supply car got pummeled through no fault of its own.

Later in the day, the most dependable horses were chosen for ferrying the materials to the railhead. All of us stumped for Blind Thomas, yet at the mention of his name, Mr. Strobridge drew back. He couldn't entrust any part of this undertaking to a sightless creature. Patrick and Jesse and I, and even some of the Celestials, I think, argued for it. We all said he was the best railcar horse there was and the hardest working, bar none. Even said we wouldn't work without him, and I know that irked Mr. Strobridge, because I saw his jaw clamp as tight as a vise.

You'd think he'd be more tolerant, considering he had but one good eye himself and the Central Pacific Railroad had promoted him to construction manager.

But because he couldn't risk another strike on a day as important as this one, we won out. And so Blind Thomas would deliver the rails from the supply car to the end of the track and keep them coming at speed.

As long as he had a rider. Yes, in the past he'd delivered the rails himself, but there was no room for error on this day. If we wanted him in on the action, Mr. Strobridge said, he'd have to have a rider. And that rider would be me.

I ducked into the meal line to grab a bowl of beans, then hurried to get Thomas ready. Brina trotted at my hip, licking her lips and looking hopeful. I tried to eat as I walked, my legs feeling as shaky as pudding. So much was riding on this day, so to speak, that my stomach began protesting its breakfast. See, what I hadn't mentioned when we'd all campaigned for Blind Thomas was this: I'd never actually ridden a horse. Sure and I'd grown up around plenty of horses in the city—the wagon horses that delivered the milk and the coal, the ones that pulled the public street cars, even the neighborhood firehorses and police horses—but they'd been good for a pat on a whiskery nose or a slobbery lapping after a bit of apple. That high section stretching between mane and tail was strictly foreign territory to me.

Blind Thomas nickered when he heard me coming. I kept my whinnies to myself and set about feeding and watering him, then grooming him to a gleam while he ate. Couldn't finish eating my own breakfast, though, and, knowing my bunkmates would curse me for it, dumped out the beans for Brina. With trembling fingers I fastened the harness into place, then fumbled with the saddle.

"Here, you've got the thing too far back." Patrick, having appeared out of nowhere, reached past me to reposition the small army saddle closer to Thomas's mane. Obviously he knew his way around a horse better than I did, which is something I hadn't known about him, so I stepped aside as he secured the girth and, after measuring me with a practiced eye, adjusted the length of the stirrups.

"Thank you," I said. "I'm owing you for that."

He clapped me on the shoulder and smiled. "You two make us proud today, all right?"

Hammer blows preceded an earsplitting rattle and crash that sent Brina scurrying aside. Rails were being off-loaded. Mr. Crocker and Mr. Strobridge had begun preparing for this battle several days ago, ordering extra materials brought by locomotive to the front and, when they arrived, sending for more. Now the bulging cars loomed like their own lengthy mountain range in the gloom. Today was full-out war: not only man against nature but man against man.

"Is it true Mr. Crocker bet ten thousand dollars we could do it?" The enormous number further knotted my stomach.

Patrick nodded. "That's the story. Heard he bet some bigwig on the U.P. that we'd lay ten miles of rail today and then some."

"But *ten thousand dollars*!"

"Oh, that's just pocket change for the likes of him. Probably lights his cigars with ten-dollar bills." He shook his head. "The thing is, the man won't even have to break a sweat to win his money."

Somebody hollered in the distance, and Patrick straightened. "I'd better be on my way." Giving me a wink, he added, "We can do this, Malachy. *Ádh mór ort.*" And he hurried off.

There was another crash and a chorus of men's shouts, and Blind Thomas lifted his head. He paused his chewing. The muscles in his neck bulged, and barley dribbled from his jaws. The fever of excitement had found its way inside him, too. He seemed to sense what the day would require. "It's going to take a mighty effort," I told him, laying a hand on his neck, which was already damp with sweat. And I passed along Patrick's Irish blessing: *"Ádh mór ort."* Good luck to you.

With the saddle and harness in place, I led Blind Thomas toward the railhead, having to push our way through the gathering crowd. Right off, I spotted the portly Mr. Crocker. He was eyeing his pocket watch and scowling like a demon, not because of any delays in the morning but because of the taunts being flung at him from the suited rapscallions standing at his rear—Union Pacific rapscallions, I surmised. Here to mock our effort.

A steam whistle shrieked, and the crowd quieted. Feet shuffled, coughs subsided. Then, quite unexpectedly and like a trumpeter's call to the battlefield, Blind Thomas let forth an exuberant whinny. Approving laughter and some applause swept the gathering. Even Mr. Crocker allowed a smile to cross his face as he raised his arm, held it motionless while he marked the hand sweeping around his watch, then dropped it.

A resounding crash and clatter startled the desert awake as metal fishplates, along with kegs of bolts and spikes, were flung from the supply car in rapid succession. The cacophony escalated as pins were released and huge iron rails tumbled onto the sand. Soon two miles' worth of materials, enough to get us started, were piled high in the gray light, and the supply car backed away so that another heavily laden car could pull forward.

To my surprise I saw that Ducks was a member of the crew lifting the first flatcar onto the tracks and loading it with sixteen rails and the necessary supplies. That unsettled me a bit. But I was too focused on hoisting myself onto Blind Thomas's broad back to give him much thought.

Lord, I was excited—nervous and excited both, and Thomas, of course, was too. He arched his neck and pranced, shook his head, and tugged the reins right out of my hands. I grabbed hold of the saddle. Grit crunched beneath his iron shoes. The power inside him built and built, and before I knew it he'd ducked his head between his forelegs and released an explosive buck.

My face slammed into his neck as I pitched forward, my nose taking the brunt of it. I felt like I'd been punched. Thomas squealed like a spirited colt while hopping around stiff legged, and it was all I could do to clamp my legs to his sides and try to gather the reins. Far away, someone hooted. But the blood rushed to my ears, and all I was aware of was the harness creaking and the stirrups banging my shins and the saddle smacking my backside whenever I chanced to make contact with it.

And then he stopped. Planted all four legs and looked around, blowing air. Gave himself a hard, allover shake, which almost knocked me loose again, and strode into his position in front of the flatcar. My legs were trembling like they had the ague, and I think my teeth may have been chattering too. All I know is, I had a death grip on the reins now, as well as on Thomas's mane, and I wasn't letting go.

The rail foreman ran a long rope from the car and fastened it to Blind Thomas's harness. Thomas shook his head and snorted, then took a step forward to tighten the rope, testing the weight behind him. "Hold up there," the foreman said to me, and Thomas obeyed. I looked over my shoulder as the loading was finished.

"Okay!" the man shouted. Brina barked and Thomas leapt forward. For a couple of heartbeats he scrambled, his hooves digging into the grit, his shoulders driving into the harness, but then the flatcar began to give way. The wheels rolled, fast and smooth, then faster and faster, and Thomas was charging along the grade to where the rails ended. This was only a short distance, as the morning was young, and he came to a stop all by himself—was I really needed?—and the eight rail layers jumped into position.

Like a well-oiled machine, they worked in partnership: four men on the left of the track and four men on the right. Clamping their tongs around a rail each, the teams ran it forward and off the car and set it in place across the wooden ties. Returned for two more and set them in place. Ahead, men were setting out more wooden ties, the rungs to a ten-mile-long ladder.

Behind us, the Celestials began handing out the necessary number of spikes and bolts and fishplates to each end of the rails, while a severe man who looked like a reverend ordered minor changes in alignment before nodding approval. In rapid succession the spikes were driven and the fishplates fastened. Blind Thomas walked forward, masterfully pacing himself with the work, and I looked over my shoulder to see another team of men leveling the ties, tamping them securely into place, and filling the intervening spaces with ballast.

In what seemed like moments the flatcar was empty. The rope was unfastened, and the Celestials swarmed in to tip the car off the rails. Another horse pulling a car of sixteen rails was coming down the newly laid track. I turned Blind Thomas around to let the other horse pass, then waited as the empty car was tipped back onto the track and the rope refastened. One of the Celestials slapped Thomas on the rump, and he bolted forward. My head jerked back and my feet came out of the stirrups again, but somehow I managed to cling to the saddle. Upon returning to the stack of supplies, I got Thomas turned around again and waited as sixteen more rails were loaded.

As if he could count, the instant number sixteen was loaded Thomas was driving into the harness and building speed. Galloping on the narrow dirt path beside the rails and then straining to keep ahead of the car as its smooth iron wheels built speed, we galloped past the previous car, tipped and waiting, and delivered the next set of rails.

I pulled on the reins, but it was like Blind Thomas knew inside his head how far he had to go, and he rushed right up to where the last pair of rails was being spiked and came to an abrupt halt. The teams clamped on their tongs and the half-ton rails began sliding off the car.

All that morning, we delivered loads of metal to feed the great Irish beast that was inching its way east across the desert floor. Spike, *ping!* Hammer, *clang! Grunt* and *thunk* and *thud.* The dry desert air vibrated under the ring of our weapons, and a heady aroma of human sweat and beaten metal perfumed the dust.

The sun climbed high and seared our faces. The wind blew and sucked the sweat from our skin and our lips. Wagons rumbled to the front, delivering water, and I looked down to find the ladle handed to me by none other than Ducks—and wasn't that a reversal, since I'd been the one to deliver his tea back near Cisco. He gave me a solemn nod of acknowledgment, dribbled some water on Thomas's sweaty face, and continued down the line.

Our Irish pounded on: two miles, two and a half, four miles, five. The reserve crew waited at the ready, but the eight shook their heads. An invisible harness held them together, and an unseen whip urged them forward. Step after determined step, boots bit into dirt, iron punctured ties, and wheels rolled across virgin rails pointed due east.

The gallop back to the supply cars grew longer

and longer. Each trip found the pop-eyed Mr. Crocker pacing himself into a lather while testing the limits of the hinge on his pocket watch. Foremen passed each other at a run, relaying messages, calling for more supplies, consulting their work sheets. Mr. Strobridge urged us on with thunderous shouts of encouragement laced with his usual profanities. But by late morning they all gave way to that invisible force that pushed us on to an effort even greater than they could demand.

My butt ached by that point. The saddle had rubbed raw spots into my legs that oozed right through the fabric of my pants. And as the day wore on the improbability of our goal settled in and things began to go wrong. The iron head of a sledge flew off, nearly decking a fellow. One of the flatcars jumped the tracks, and its ungainly load of rails spilled across the desert floor. Ties shifted and splintered. We worked at such speed that our empty flatcar was once tipped from the track before Blind Thomas was unfastened from it, and the tightening rope yanked him off balance. He grunted alarm and fought to stay on his feet as he was pulled, staggering, backward. I grabbed hold of his mane and hunched as we began to go down. Someone shouted and, I think, slapped Thomas on the rump, because he suddenly gave another great effort and heaved himself upright onto the grade, where he stood snorting gusts of air. I was trembling so violently,

I could barely look over my shoulder to see what had happened. To my surprise Ducks stood with a knife in one hand and the severed rope in the other. Triumph lit his face. Guilt must have burned across mine.

The work hurtled onward, and when one thirty came and six miles were measured, Mr. Crocker called for a lunch break. He called for fresh horses and fresh men, too, but the eight tracklayers shook off their replacements. I happily slid from Blind Thomas's back and began to unhitch him, but he pinned his ears and refused to move away from his flatcar. He leaned all his weight back toward the car, in fact, as stubborn as a mule. Rather than delay the work, the foreman signaled me to hitch him up again. Wearily, I pulled myself into the saddle, and we headed down the track with another load of rails.

The sun crested the sky and began to sink at our backs, and something in the air shifted. We all felt it. Nature had witnessed what we could do and was retreating, giving up. The day was ours to make a mark for all time.

And so the Irish fought on, even though the effort was taking its toll. Sledges swung at a slower clip, requiring ever-louder groans to hoist them into the air. Shoulders knotted, hands blistered. Trickling sweat and grime and insects conspired to blind us from the finish. But the Irish fought on.

And then it was dusk and dark and we were done.

and George, and over there
d and the others. Two foremen
er, conversing in hushed voices.
g of history. Eight Irish heroes
mes into the tablets of time.

inning, I looked around to see
hind us, I spotted Ducks and his
rcle of their own and looking just
ing his eye, I impulsively lifted a
done it! He took a moment to form
his arm and added a polite nod. He
ords, but all at once I knew what he
sands of men had contributed to this
ery day. Back in the mountains, in fact,
n had also given their all. They'd given
ir names would never make the history

dusk. There were Edward

Michael Kennedy and Fre

squatted beside each oth

We all sensed the maki

had just carved their na

Unable to stop g

who else was near. Be

crew squatting in a ci

as bone weary. Catc

fist in triumph: we'd

a like fist, then lifted

didn't mouth any w

was thinking: Thous

day as they did ev

eight Chinese me

their lives. But the

books.

in

ov

Mary

tons o.

"T

just mea

"It's i

"I kno

by the U.P.,

was a miracl

He closed his

Brina dive

in her own celel

grimy brow, I san

In every direc

desert floor, their e

Twenty-Nine

I'll admit I walked with a swagger after that. Ten miles
of rail had been laid in one day, and every ounce of it—
every ounce and pound and ton of it—had been hoisted
and set in place by an Irishman. I was clapped on the
back and included in the commendations, which put a
decided spring in my step. Blind Thomas, too, was celebrated as a hero. Instant genealogies traced him (through
willful fancy and whiskey reckoning) back to solid Irish
stock. No horse could have pulled so tirelessly without a
few drops of Irish blood coursing through his veins. And
wasn't "Thomas" itself a good Irish name? The very next
day, a trio of high-spirited men delivered a pint of beer
to him at supper and, proving his loyalties, he licked his
bucket clean.

Less than half a dozen miles to Promontory Summit
now, and we were eager to finish the work begun five

and a half years ago: daunting, backbreaking work that had crossed five hundred desert miles, bored fifteen granite tunnels, and survived countless storms and snow slides. But word came down that the bigwigs from the two railroads were arguing about the details of the joining-up ceremony, and so, incongruously, the rail construction— so close to the finish—slowed.

The other thing putting a gimp in my swagger was the presence of Ducks. We were living in neighboring camps again, and sitting on the gold that had once been the Celestials' wages was poking at me harder than ever. More and more, when I happened upon him during the day, I flinched like I was seeing a ghost. He always nodded acknowledgment, but his flat, emotionless mask aggravated me. I wanted to shake him! I wanted to lift a fist and demand, "What are you thinking? What, if anything, do you know?"

Nothing, I calmed myself. He knew nothing. I was fairly sure of it.

But he looked thinner, bonier. Was his peaked appearance my fault?

No, it wasn't. Not when you examined the particulars. If he and his fellow Celestials had agreed to eat the boiled beef and beans that the railroad served, then they wouldn't need extra money for food. To my mind, anyone who demanded to eat pickled fish parts and dried roots and tinned oysters, and had to have such delicacies sent all the way from San Francisco, *should* have to pay extra. So his condition wasn't my fault. What it came down to was, you had to look out for yourself these days. Every man did. Root, hog, or die.

But then in my mind rose the image, as bold as brass, of him holding the knife and the cut rope, when he'd saved Blind Thomas and me from likely disaster. He'd been looking out for us, when he certainly didn't have to.

Yes, well, that was a choice he'd made, so that needn't change my reasoning. It wasn't my fault.

It seemed, though, that each time I merely nudged my haversack, the coins hidden inside clinked accusation. Every ear in the car pricked, too, I was certain, and every head solemnly nodded agreement: guilty.

My torment grew such that one afternoon when I was walking along the tracks, my footsteps began crunching a rhythm that carried me back to the kitchen of my childhood—the kitchen where my ma instructed us in the Ten Commandments, our recitations accompanied by the sharp clang of her spoon against the soup pot. *Thou shalt not steal*, I heard her say. *Thou shalt not steal*, I heard myself repeat, innocently and earnestly, with no real understanding of the ways of the world. *Clang. Thou shalt not steal*, she said again for emphasis. *Thou shalt* not *steal*, I repeated, unaware at that youthful age that looking out for yourself and your family meant pocketing what happened to come your way. *Clang.*

It wasn't my fault that Ducks had been blamed.

Yet that day, the spikers seemed to hammer home the identical message, with each ringing clang of the sledge echoing a stroke to the soup pot: *Thou . . . shalt . . . not . . . steal. Thou . . . shalt . . .* not *. . . steal.* Bolts spilled to the ground with the clatter of enormous coins, and I flinched.

I got knotted inside because the litany bored into my brain and wouldn't give over, and every time I turned, it seemed, I came face-to-face with Ducks. There was Ducks helping align the rail ahead of me. There was Ducks reaching for the same bucket of nails, our fists knocking atop the handle. There was Ducks heading toward his camp, crossing my path as I headed toward mine. Always wearing his emotionless mask.

So twisted and sleepless did I become, early one morning I plunged my fist to the bottom of my haversack, ready to hand over the coins to him and be done with the matter, and my fingers closed instead around the latest letter from my ma: The rent was two months overdue; Dr. Flaherty was still owed $2.60; Sean needed new boots— *again*; and don't worry about her, the lingering cough was nothing really, her cross to bear, nothing, she was sure of it, to worry about. That pile of gold I was holding on to would certainly deliver some much-needed sunshine to my family.

"What's gnawing at ye?" Patrick asked on the way to breakfast. I only gave him a shrug and walked toward the meal line, certain that every head marked my passing. The relief of the confessional was not to be mine.

What I was thinking was this: Wasn't the commandment about stealing near the end of the list, number seven or eight, at least? Certainly it wasn't God's most important rule. Certainly he knew his people had to pay rent, pay the doctor, pay the grocer and the seamstress and the coal man. He knew I had a family to look after. It was a man's job. And it wasn't as if I'd killed anybody. That commandment was much higher on the list.

In striding toward my food, eyes to the ground and not paying attention, I plowed full on into someone: Ducks, of course. I scrambled for balance and to recover my falling hat, finally found my feet, and continued. The irritating impression I carried with me was that he wasn't anywhere near as shaken as I was.

Thirty

Low clouds canopied the sky. The air, muggy and uncomfortable, weighed heavily. Here we were, finally, at Promontory Summit, waiting for the Union Pacific to bring their rails to the finish, and doing little more than twiddling our thumbs. And the Central Pacific, without the joining-up even completed, was already dismantling. There simply wasn't enough work left for the thousands of us on the payroll so, seeing no future (and no gold), men were packing up and climbing aboard the emptied supply trains headed back west. Half the bunks in our sleeping car now lay vacant, the floor littered with muddied and unmatched gloves, crusted tins, broken laces, and forgotten caps. The lingering odor of sweat mocked us; it reeked of an unclaimed prize.

Being at loose ends didn't sit well with those of us who remained, and tensions ran just below the skin. What was going to happen to us? Rumors were flying that both railroads were out of money and that we might not get paid at all, even for the labor we'd already done, and that set some jaws, I'm telling you.

Maybe those same tensions were snaking through the Chinese camps, because something started an all-out brawl one day, with several hundred jumping into the fight. Guns were pulled—which surprised me, because I hadn't known any of the peaceable Celestials even owned guns—and Mr. Strobridge and his men had to ride in and crack a few heads. Several of the Celestials got shot, I heard, and one was lingering somewhere, not expected to live. It just went to show that you could never fully trust those people because you never knew what they were thinking.

A few of us, including Patrick and Jesse and I, discussed it and decided we'd worked too hard not to stay around long enough to see the last spike driven. So with the ceremony scheduled for the next day, May 8, and nothing tying us to camp, we strolled toward the row of large canvas constructions calling itself Promontory. Brina, of course, trotted alongside.

None of us spoke the words, but I saw how pride squared our shoulders as we began mingling with the throng of onlookers. The eyes and ears of the entire nation, after all, were focused on this one spot, as proved by the telegraph wires nailed onto poles that marched toward the big cities in the east and the west. We'd played our part.

Despite the glowering sky, the mood in Promontory was bubbly. Word must have spread like a wildfire, because people were traveling in from all over to witness history. Farmers and prospectors, cowboys and salesmen, soldiers and even ordinary families with their children peeking button-eyed from the backs of wagons, crowded their way past the tents. Locomotives, gleaming in their brilliant red and blue and green colors, arrived from both directions to disgorge a swarm of dignitaries who all lifted champagne bottles and whooped in celebration. Reporters scribbled furiously in their notebooks. Photographers scurried to the edges of the chaos like black beetles, lugging their accordion cameras and bulky tripods from platform to hillock to ladder—even to the rooftop of a moving supply train—seeking to claim the most advantageous site for recording tomorrow's event.

There being no entertainment in Promontory until that event, the crowds flocked into the newly erected tents as into a church on Sunday—except that the people beckoning to us from inside the flaps dressed nothing like black-robed priests. The canvas panels took on a life of their own as they bulged with elbows and strained to encompass shoulders. When the clamorous festivities reached a fever pitch, too much for the tents to hold, celebrants found themselves spit out onto the dirt street. Smiling, they dusted themselves off and stumbled toward another tent.

It wasn't long before Jesse and Patrick, lured by a wink and a smile, dived into one saloon with the advertisement RED CLOUD painted across it. Of course I wanted to follow (I was real curious), but dogs weren't allowed inside for one, and two, I needed to see if Promontory had set up a post office yet. If they had, I was about ready to carry in the gold coins I'd been hiding and exchange them for a postal money order to be sent to my family in New York. Maybe stealing it had been wrong, but living so close to Ducks while having to hide it was unbearable. He'd already paid the railroad back, I figured, with his year of work, so now it really wouldn't matter if I sent it off to my family. The rent would be caught up, the doctor paid, shoes and food and fabric for clothes bought. Ma could even get herself some horehound candy to ease her cough. The load, at last, would be lifted.

Just as I began my search, though, I was nearly flattened by three men jostling their way past the canvas opening of a neighboring tent. Their colorful swearing betrayed their Irish birth, and their grimy clothes identified them as railroad men. Right away, I pegged them as coming from the other line, because the U.P. workers had a particular reputation.

"It's but a wee bit of sport," one was arguing, and something in his tone made me cock an ear. The man's freckled face, nearly as ruddy as his hair, had the misfortune to be crowned by a brow so crooked it had fixed itself into a permanent scowl. Below that scowl, a stubby nose bent to one side. Everything about him seemed off-kilter, in fact, including his bowlegged gait. "Be a grand thing, wouldn't it, now," he said, traveling a short loop, "to flush ourselves a few coolies—maybe blow a few of the buggers back to China, where they belong?" A lopsided grin split his face as he answered his own question. "Aye, that might suit, boys, it just might." Coming to a wavering stop, he peered through the crowds. "Sure and there's no need to look far, is there? The C.P. is crawling with the yellow monkeys." He gave an exaggerated shudder. "It's a regular infestation, it is."

"Aye, that it is," replied one of his mates, still bracing himself against the tent frame but squinting into the distance. "Let's have a stop in Conner's and discuss it."

"No, no, no," protested Bowlegs, swatting the air. "I said it's an infrus . . . infres . . . infestation. Can't let these pesky pests take over." He dug for something in his pocket.

"Of course we can't, but—"

"And we won't!" he proclaimed, holding up a small object for inspection. "God bless us, we're going to help with the spring cleaning." He lowered his voice to a conspiratorial whisper. "Along with Sheriff Nitro here."

Nitro? He was carrying nitroglycerin in his pocket? The man was crazy, entirely devoid of his senses. Nitro was as unpredictable as a rattler and a hundred times as deadly. We'd tried using the invention back in the mountains once, and it had exploded before it was supposed to, collapsing the wrong wall, splintering the dump cart, and sending the chemist back to Sacramento with a severe limp. Thank the Lord I'd unhitched Blind Thomas in advance and moved him far away from the scene. That's when the foreman decided to stick with black powder. It wasn't as powerful, maybe, but it was a world easier to control.

"Mind yourself!" the other friend exclaimed, lunging to keep Bowlegs from losing his balance. "You're apt to get us all killed. Here now, mightn't you let Gerald take it?"

"No." Bowlegs clutched the small container to his chest and examined his friend like he was meeting him for the first time. "You're an ugly bugger, you know that? It's your teeth. Your ma get frightened by a rabbit when she was big with ye?"

The friend, ignoring the insult, took hold of Bowlegs's

elbow. "Come along now. Hand it over and I'll buy you another drink, I will."

"No!" Bowlegs shook himself free. "Ye haven't got the training. My cousin's a chemist—with a college degree. He mixed this oil himself. 'Tis only a few drops, but it's enough to give some coolies their wings." Then he plunged unsteadily into the crowd, waving one arm. "C'mon, you Nancies, let's have some sport."

The two looked at each other and shook their heads but followed in his wake.

My heart was banging in my chest. This couldn't end well. What should I do? I didn't wish harm on any of the Celestials, but what could *I* do? Squashing the warning that pricked my insides, I began to tag along—until I glanced over my shoulder and saw Brina sitting stubbornly in place, forcing people to step around her. She had her yellow eyes pinned narrowly on me, delivering judgment. There wasn't time to argue with her now. Slapping my leg, I called, "Brina, come!"

She didn't so much as blink.

"Brina, *come! Come!*"

Refusing to hide her opinion of this venture, she finally rose to her feet and took her time stalking toward me. When she'd almost covered the distance, I turned and hurried after the three U.P. men.

In all the months I'd worked for the railroad I'd never

actually entered one of the Chinese camps; I'd never had the need, and it felt too much like trespassing. Even now, I hung back as the three stood beside an empty tent, whispering and sniggering like overgrown schoolboys on a lark. Again a wave of unease soured my stomach. Should I try to warn the Celestials? Get help? Try to stop these three? Taking a mental measurement of their collective brawn, I knew that would prove futile.

Maybe nothing would happen. There'd been talk about chasing the Celestials out of the country for more than a year now, but nothing ever came of it. Talk was just talk.

At least most of the camp was empty. A few dozen Celestials clustered in groups, drinking tea and chatting. One man fished dripping laundry from a barrel and wrung it out, piece by piece. Beneath a shade cloth, a particularly large group hunched around a game, probably the one with the cup and the dried beans. Voices swelled at that moment and broke like a wave, sounding both joy and dismay, and several of the players left the game, some shaking their heads, others counting their coins. One of these was Ducks, and he was smiling broadly while clutching his winnings. Suddenly I wanted to warn him. I owed him that much.

There was a scrabbling at my feet as Brina, recognizing Ducks, bounded happily toward him. At the same instant, Bowlegs let out a shrill whistle that caused all the Celestials to look in our direction. His arm coiled backward, building momentum. *No!*

But I didn't say it, I only thought it. His two friends turned and shielded their faces as I sprinted past them. *No, no!* And finally, out loud: *"Stop!"* Too late. Like a lashing whip, the arm jerked forward, the vial arced into the air. . . . There was Brina. . . . There was Ducks, hugging her. . . . His gaze leapt from her to me to the hurled explosive. . . . He curled his body around her. . . . And then a blinding flash accompanied an earsplitting bang. An invisible punch lifted me into the air and knocked me cold.

Time fell apart, and as through the stupor of a dream, I found myself climbing onto my hands and knees, my chest searching for air and my ears ringing. I gazed at the scene. Bodies lay scattered in every direction, like the cast-off playthings of some monstrous children. Tattered tents fluttered weakly in the residual breeze. Ash and dust swirled silently.

At the fringes of my consciousness people came running, shouting, and I tried to blink away the fog, tried to make sense of this. Where was Ducks? (Jesus, my head hurt!) Where was Brina?

Some of the bodies began stirring. Moans underpinned the shouts. But other bodies remained motion-

Thirty-One

When you've killed somebody, people look at you
differently. You come walking up, and the sea of people
parts like you're Moses (he of the commandments)
because you've performed an act of biblical gravity.
Then again, maybe I had it wrong. Maybe people drew
back because I was like one of those lepers from the
Bible stories, cast out from society and made to cry
"unclean, unclean."

My gut twisted into knots. It didn't seem to occur to
anyone that I'd not actually attacked the Celestials' camp.
I was only standing near the attackers when it happened.

Patrick reached across the chasm that evening.
"You were just in the wrong place at the wrong time,"
he said, not quite looking me in the eye. So how much
did he believe his own words? "'Twas an accident. You
didn't mean to be there."

less. Dead? They were dead? *Where was Ducks?*

Thou shalt not kill. That higher commandment burst into my brain. Guilt delivered a kick to my gut. The talk wasn't just talk; it hadn't stopped at words. And I hadn't acted fast enough, hadn't spoken up soon enough.

Oh, Jesus, Mary, and Joseph! Where were Ducks and Brina?

Thou shalt not kill. Oh, God, I'd done it.

I tried to nod my thanks before he turned away, but that nagging voice inside me probed: *Didn't* I mean to be there? Hadn't I followed the U.P. men to see what would happen, when I could all too easily guess the outcome?

Jesse, after spitting a stream of his tobacco juice and giving a shrug, made light of the situation. "What difference does it make? You haven't put no more than a dent in their population." He scratched his ear. "I do miss Brina, though."

I wanted to climb out of my skin.

The joining-up ceremony didn't happen the next day, Saturday, as it was supposed to. The clouds opened and let a hard rain pour down with a vengeance. It was still raining come Sunday. On tired horses and tattered tents, on iron rails and the unclaimed relics of shattered bodies. Officials from the Union Pacific Railroad telegraphed that they couldn't even make it to the site, so the ceremony was put on hold. Rumor had it that the delay was due more to guns than weather, that angry U.P. workers who were owed a load of back pay were holding the train hostage. Meanwhile, Promontory wallowed in a sea of mud.

When I could no longer stand the furtive glances and suspicious whispering that multiplied throughout camp, I flipped up my collar, tugged on my cap, and slogged through the rain and the mud to find Blind Thomas. Instinctively I braced for Brina's exuberant lunge to my hip, her busy tongue slobbering my hand. But only a distinct void shadowed me, and aching with that emptiness, I continued alone.

Blind Thomas stood with the other horses, head down, patiently waiting out the weather. I sidled up to his shoulder, announcing my presence with a murmur, and laid a wet hand beneath his stringy mane. He lifted his head and arced it around. Locating my shoulder, he nuzzled it gently. Then he bobbed his head, pulling me in. His thick lips felt as warm as fingers, affectionate, nonjudgmental. Tears filled my eyes. Good old Blind Thomas. Faithful Thomas. So selfishly grateful was I for his blindness then, because I couldn't have borne it if he'd looked at me as so many others now did.

That hadn't stopped Ducks from looking at me in that way. Over and over in my mind, his final look of shock and sharp disappointment shot through me, his flash of awareness that I was less than he'd thought. He'd seen me standing beside the man throwing the explosive, and he'd gone to his grave believing I hated him. When I didn't.

Nor could I stop revisiting the way Ducks, in his last breath, had tried to shield Brina from the blast. Poor, poor Brina, who hadn't even been asked if she wanted to come on this trek, and yet I'd put a rope around her neck—which had become a noose now, hadn't it—and dragged her here to her death.

That's when I cried. Couldn't help it.

It was later on that same afternoon that Mr. Strobridge sent for me.

I trudged through the rain again, this time like I was going to my own hanging. Which I was.

Mr. Strobridge kept his office in the same railcar where he lived. I'd never been inside and didn't care to have the privilege now, so it was with a heart sunk low that I pulled myself up the steps. A good part of me was hoping he'd been called away, but there he sat, of course, his towering frame bent over the storm of papers strewn across his desk. A brass lamp cast a puddle of yellow light on his work, and that made a warm contrast to the cold, gray skies pressing against the curtained window. Within reach of his large, calloused hands sat an incongruously dainty teacup and saucer, and beside it, a matching pot hooded by a cozy. Although several chairs, straight backed and cloth covered, dressed the room, I was so dripping and muddy that I stood in the entry until he finally lifted his head and motioned me forward. Beyond the wall came the animated sound of women's voices— one of them his wife, no doubt—and the clatter of pots and lids. I smelled a good Irish stew cooking. That aroma called to me something fierce, and I was a child again.

Mr. Strobridge let me just stand there, and I waited, thoroughly miserable, as his black eye patch, judge and jury both, measured me up and down. The verdict was soon rendered: Found wanting. Lacking a backbone or any character. Lacking a voice.

"Mr. Gormley, is it?"

I nodded. (*"Gorm Li?"* I heard Ducks echo from far in the past. *"Li is Chinese name."*) Some little brother I'd turned out to be.

"We count five Chinese dead, one missing, and three injured in your shenanigans of Friday last. In addition, one laborer for the U.P. is dead. Since it appears he was the one who hurled the nitroglycerin, his rightful punishment has already been delivered."

The number of deaths shocked me anew. I hadn't meant—hadn't meant . . . what?

"Those two other hooligans at the scene are being handled by the U.P. As for you, your employment with the Central Pacific is terminated. The wages due you for your last two weeks will instead be handed over to the Chinese to help cover the expenses of shipping the dead back to their families."

This was the time to give back the gold coins. They rightfully belonged to Ducks and the others. The money could be used to ship home Ducks's body, if the pieces of it could be gathered.

"Do you have anything to say on your behalf?"

Say? I moved my jaw, but the words wouldn't come—as usual. They never arrived in time. More and more often, it seemed, I stood by and let others speak. Even when it was wrong. Burning with shame, I shook my head.

Mr. Strobridge pushed back his chair and eyed me with undisguised distaste. "Nothing at all?"

I didn't mean to! I wanted to cry. *I tried to stop it.*

"We couldn't have come this far without them, you know. The Chinamen."

I nodded agreement. It didn't seem enough, and it wasn't.

He studied me longer, giving me the chance to say something, anything, in my defense, but misery held me mute.

"Pack your things," he said at last, and jerked his head toward the door.

I stepped out into a colder rain.

Since all the trains were coming toward Promontory and none were heading back until after the joining-up ceremony, I had at least a couple of long days to wait. A lot of hours to kill. So that night after supper, feeling itchy and willfully reckless, I joined the poker game in our sleeping car. Jesse dealt the cards, as usual, and the betting proceeded, as usual, but something was different. During my afternoon absence, something seemed to have been decided and an invisible curtain had been pulled between the others and me. They now communicated wordlessly, through confederated expressions and subtle cues, and I didn't have the code.

I'm not saying they were cheating—I'm not—though the cards dealt me that night stood so far apart, they might as well have been warring. No two cards would pair up or even line up. Hand after hand, I drew scattered small numbers and mixed suits. But I couldn't drop out of the game; *I couldn't.* I had to belong somewhere. And so, even though I was losing a whole lot more money than I had, I kept right on betting.

The funny thing was, it was as if everyone at the table knew I was in over my head yet had a secret agreement to keep dealing me cards. And when it came time to toss in another coin and my pockets were empty, no one commented. Patrick just rose from his chair and sauntered over to my bunk, reached under it—while my heart clawed its way up my throat—and dragged out my haversack. *No!* He dug his hand into it and lifted out the bag of gold coins. "I think you've more than enough here to put things right."

"That's the railroad's money bag!" exclaimed one of the other men, as if reading from his script.

Jesse shook his head sadly. "It's like we never knew you, Malachy."

Thirty-Two

I snatched the bag from Patrick's hand, my face heated. Threw enough coins on the table to cover my losses and then, because it was late, climbed into my bunk. Lying there as stiff as a board, I listened to the others color me with their perceptions. Hadn't I always been a little closemouthed? Obviously I thought I was too good for them. And the way I kept to myself had been suspicious from the start. The nature of a thief. Who could you trust these days, really? A general clucking of tongues circled the table and sealed my sentence. I was cast out.

Where would I go now? The "great enterprise" was over. For the Central Pacific Railroad, for me. They could hold their ceremony, but I wouldn't be a part of it.

I dug my fists together. Man alive, I was angry! With them, with myself, with my pa—still—for leaving and getting killed. And now I'd done the killing. I was angry at the way I'd let everyone down. I wanted to punch something.

Long after the lamp was doused and the car fell silent, I lay staring into the darkness. My mind jack-rabbited from one image to another, settling nowhere. In the cavernous gloom I came to believe I could hear Brina licking her paws, that slow, monotonous slurping that had so often lulled me to sleep. Hoping for a moment that this had all been a bad dream, I lifted onto an elbow and cocked an ear. Nothing. Not even the annoyance of Patrick's snoring. The very night seemed to be holding its breath, awaiting a decision.

I flopped onto my back and trudged through the torment. Certain I could hear singing somewhere in the distance, a faint, sad voice, I lifted up again, but the melody was snuffed away at once. Such was the mind's trickery.

Hours passed with me staring dully into the gloom hovering beneath the car's ceiling. The cloudy depths pooled and eddied, then parted to reveal an inky sky. Nearly within my reach, sparkling stars danced—no, not stars: tiny lanterns pulled by a colorful kite delivering the spirits of the dead to the heavens. The lanterns' flames leapt in exuberance, giving honor.

Maybe I dozed some, or maybe the dancing lanterns

held me mesmerized, but when I came to with a jolt, I knew at once what I had to do. Everyone was still asleep so, shouldering the haversack containing my few things and the railroad's money bag, I slipped out of the car and headed for the Chinamen's camp. The desert air hung cold, but the predawn skies were clear, hinting at a coming breeze. Perfect weather.

Orange cooking fires already glowed among the white tents, and a few shadowy figures moved about. Was I known to them? Or was I just one face among many, as indistinguishable as one tent was from another? After what had happened, did every Irishman, by the mere chance of his being Irish, risk his life walking into this camp?

A sane Irishman might at least have rustled up some friends to accompany him, but I couldn't count on those right now. I had to find Mr. Chang, and so I began strolling the rows of tents alone.

A great many of them, I discovered, were already empty, cleaned out bare to the ground, while others held a few sparse furnishings but no people. Where was everybody? Spotting a cook hovering over his pot, I mustered my courage and approached him through the dark. He startled, and held his wooden spoon in instinctive defense, then shook his head at my inquiries. The same thing occurred with the next cook and then the little group of men squatted around their fire.

Did they truly not understand me, or were they stubbornly unwilling to help? Undeterred, I pushed on. Traveling farther into the camp, I surprised a man who was taking his first whiz of the morning. When I again asked for Mr. Chang's whereabouts, a hand waved me down the tracks. "Promontory," the exposed man said as he hunched his shoulders and turned away. Only too happy to end my trespassing, I hurriedly began hiking the few miles into Promontory.

Beneath the clear morning sky, Promontory was a beehive of activity. The last-spike ceremony was finally going to take place that day, Monday, May 10, and, as before, people of all kinds were crowding the tents and milling along the one dirt street fronting the tracks. That was fine for them and their champagne-swigging friends; I was planning my own ceremony: to honor Ducks, a self-named brother who'd done nothing but look out for me. I might have died if not for him, crushed by that falling tree in the Sierra Nevada or by the teetering railcar on the ten-mile day. He deserved some sort of remembrance, and I was going to provide it. And I was planning to honor Brina as well, the fairest and most honest dog that ever lived, one I hadn't deserved. (If anyone wanted to raise an eyebrow at that, I'd remind him that St. Francis himself had blessed a wolf, now, hadn't he.)

But finding Mr. Chang in this ever-expanding crowd

was going to be difficult. I zigged and zagged, searched faces, toured the outskirts of the gathering, and plunged into its middle. In stepping aside for a three-member group to pass, I ran full on into a barrel-shaped man with arms sprung away from his shoulders. A whoosh of hair tonic wafted under my nose.

"Sorry," I apologized, glancing briefly into a friendly and vaguely familiar face.

"No, I'm at fault here," he replied. "Too busy with my wafers to pay attention to where I'm traveling. Necco?" He extended the unwrapped cylinder toward me.

It was the same man who'd shared my seat on that first train ride up to the little town of Cisco. He'd offered the Neccos then, too. Did he—?

"Say, do I know you?" Frowning, he stepped back to measure me up and down.

I nodded. "We were on the same train a couple of years ago."

"To Cisco! I remember now. You're from New York, right?" Then, looking past me, he said, "Where's that fine dog of yours?"

There was so much I suddenly wanted to say to this smiling man, so much I wanted to confide, but all I could get out was, "She's gone. With a friend." And that came as a surprise, calling Ducks a friend.

"Oh." He hesitated, as if expecting me to explain

the particulars and, when I didn't, continued. "I'm John Hammond." He extended his meaty hand toward me. "Good to see you again. Remind me of your name."

"Malachy," I replied, grasping his hand and shaking it. Felt good to do so. "Malachy Gormley."

"Yes, yes." He appraised me again. "How have you found the railroad work, son? Are you enjoying it?"

"Yes, sir," I lied, both the work and the enjoyment now being terminated.

With a wink, he asked, "And you've kept clear of the fisticuffs? I seem to remember those fellows on the train riding you pretty hard."

"Yes, sir." At least that was the truth. I hadn't had to punch anyone to kill them.

He chuckled. "And now I remember that, too. You're a man of few words, aren't you, Malachy? But I'll wager that when you do speak, your words are well considered." Satisfied with his pronouncement, he made to leave. "If you'll excuse me, I need to join my friends on Mr. Stanford's train. This rail-building enterprise has proved quite challenging. We've almost come to fisticuffs ourselves on occasion. Only time will tell what fruit may come of it. Good to see you again." With a wave of his hand, one that still clutched the Neccos, he bustled off.

Hours passed as I continued my search, and the

time for the ceremony approached. Where was Mr. Chang? There were close to a thousand people now, all crowding around the spot where the two tracks would join up, though only a couple dozen, I guessed, would actually be able to see what was happening. What a hodgepodge: proper ladies who pulled in their rustling skirts to avoid the careless boots of sunburned laborers, soft-skinned gentlemen in trimmed beards who shouted over the straw hats of mute Chinamen, none of them Mr. Chang. In combing the fringes of the crowd, I thought I even saw two Indians on their ponies.

Towering above all heads were the C.P.'s brilliant blue and red locomotive, *Jupiter*, and facing it at a short distance, the U.P.'s brass-accented, gray and red No. 119. Men seeking a better view had clambered onto both engines and now swung from every available metal support like monkeys. From somewhere in that merriment came the stirring *rat-a-tat-tat* of drums that introduced the blare of military buglers. Champagne flowed like water.

With a white sun shining high in the freshly scrubbed sky, the crowd suddenly quieted. Like the ripple emanating from a stone plunked into water, hats were removed in ever-widening circles; heads bowed. Someone had called for prayer. Accustomed to my ma's threatening pinch, I pulled off my hat and stood in place. In the distance pealed the measured voice of a reverend, but I couldn't make out his words.

"What did he say?" A reporter elbowed my ribs and held up his notebook, pencil at the ready. I shook my head and shrugged. "Never mind," he said, and set to scribbling, no doubt writing the story that the nation wanted to hear. Whether it was true was another matter entirely.

In an attempt to hear the speaker, the crowd shoved forward, and I was thrown against a man's broad back.

"Hey!" he growled.

"Sorry," I replied, and squeezed behind and past him toward open air.

A different voice boomed and faded across the crowd: "greatest railroad enterprise of the world . . . hands of her citizens . . . brightest promise." Listeners applauded and cheered. Yet another man took the stage to deliver grand phrases. Then another and another. It was happening, the long-awaited union, but I couldn't hear it. Spotting some Chinamen standing off to themselves, I worked my way in that direction.

A burst of laughter shot from the front line, and the bells on both locomotives clanged with glee. What was going on? The crowd held its breath, and in the ensuing silence came the clumsy thud of a sledge having missed its target. That unleashed even more raucous laughter.

"He missed again!" someone hooted, and the bells clanged once more. It sounded like some dignitary was trying to hammer home a spike and having a hard time of it. Well, that was no surprise. Laying rail was skilled work; you didn't just step off a train and tap a spike into place with no experience. What a bunch of swellheads.

Finally the familiar ring of hammer to spike split the air, and the crowd roared. So it was done at last. The great project completed, the country now joined. Whistles shrieked madly, champagne bottles burst on all sides. The locomotives chugged to life, and I stood on my tiptoes—though I could only see the smokestacks above the crowd—as a lumbering waltz was performed. First the C.P.'s *Jupiter* reversed and politely invited the U.P.'s No. 119 to cross over onto our track, and then No. 119 returned the favor, backing up and allowing *Jupiter* to cross onto U.P. rails.

The crowd continued to cheer with unmerited abandon. Men who'd not spent a day on the rails tossed their dress hats into the air. A pair of women near me hugged each other almost to the point of suffocation and wiped tears from their eyes. The little girl holding on to her mother's skirt jumped up and down, waved her doll, and squealed like an idiot.

I shook my head and threaded my way out of the crowd. The Chinamen were disbanding, but there, finally, was Mr. Chang in his red-trimmed jacket, wiping the spectacles that hung from their braided red ribbon. Mustering my courage again, I approached.

He stiffened when he saw me. Setting his spectacles firmly in place, he said, "What do *you* want?"

So he knew the role I'd had in the deaths of his countrymen. He was wrathful, and rightfully so. But I noted the breach in his wall. Even given the immense injustice, as well as the advantage he had over me in age, he was wary. My being white was still the high card, and one Mr. Chang would never hold.

I didn't play it.

"I'm sorry," I began, my heart thumping. "I tried to stop them. I tried to—"

He waved away my apologies and clung to his anger. "I repeat: What do you want?"

Shoving my hands in my pockets, I took a deep breath. "Two things. Did Ducks have—"

"Who?"

Oh, that's right. "Ducks" wasn't his real name. What was it? Madly I tried to think, because Mr. Chang was folding the papers he carried and preparing to leave. The name had something to do with quacking. "Chun . . . quack . . ."

"Chun Kwok Keung?"

"That's him! I want to know if—"

"Yes," he answered before I could finish, "he has your dog. But I don't know where."

Of course he didn't. Brina and Ducks were both dead. As soon as I delivered the gold coins I was going to ask Mr. Chang about getting a kite and some of those tiny lanterns. "Did he say if he had kin in your camp? I have something for them." I wanted to make certain the money went to Ducks's family.

"No, there's no family here. Only an uncle in Sacramento, I think. He headed east."

"The uncle?"

"No! *Keung* headed east." He shook his head. "I offered him good money to stay. Sometime he makes the troubles, but he is a smart worker. Other men like him. Your dog likes him, I noticed."

What was he talking about? "I don't understand. Who is headed east?"

"Keung and your dog. Isn't that what you asked?" He pressed his glasses to the bridge of his nose and blinked at me.

I worked my jaw, confusion robbing me of words. "I thought that . . . They're not . . . They're alive?"

He shrugged. "They were alive when they left our camp. It was the same day as the attack . . . by you and your . . . friends." I cringed at being roped into that group. "He left saying the ancestors had told him to travel east."

"They're alive?" A surging joy nearly blinded me. "And those men weren't my friends—they weren't! They're really alive?"

"He is alive now. But Chun Kwok Keung is one we call *zhuo bak yut mung*, he has his head in the clouds." He pursed his lips in disapproval. "He needs to spend more time watching his feet than the stars, watch where his feet are traveling. I worry for him."

"What do you mean? Why?"

Mr. Chang folded his arms. "Do you think a lone Chinaman will find welcome in your American cities? It is okay with you that we work on this railroad, pick your fruit, wash your laundry. But we are not allowed in your eating houses, we cannot put our money in your banks, we cannot bring a case of injustice to a white man's court of law." He clamped his lips, biting back the greater part of what he'd like to say. In his roiling eyes I saw the indignation of a man who had twisted himself into the proper image of an American, one who could talk and dress like one but who would never be accepted as an equal. "Keung, with his head in the clouds, will not see this." Making a motion to leave, he concluded, "He will meet with a not-happy end."

"Did he say where he was going exactly?"

Mr. Chang shook his head. "He is . . . inscrutable."

I didn't even know what that meant, but somehow it

suited Ducks. In listening to Mr. Chang my curiosity had been tickled, so I had to ask, "Where did you learn to speak English like that?"

He bowed his head as if recalling a long-hidden memory. "I will tell you." Taking a deep breath, he said, "When I was four years old, I was adopted by a Baptist family in Baltimore." He paused, seemingly carried back in time, and when he continued, spoke from a far-off place. "I remember they stood me outside on their porch and cut off my hair and burned my clothes. Then they dressed me in their son's clothes, which were too big, and sat me at their table. I was so hungry, and I had never in my life seen so much food. *Are all Americans so wealthy?* I remember thinking." At his side he began shaking a finger in agitation. "The lady who adopted me held up each plate and bowl and named its food. I was instructed to repeat her words." His finger shook harder, scolding. "Immediately, and ever after, if I wanted to eat that food, I had to ask for it by its English name. No pointing; pointing is for monkeys." Catching himself, he folded his fingers into a fist and looked up. "If I couldn't ask in English, I couldn't eat. Hunger, you see, is a very good teacher."

Thirty-Three

Mr. Chang, having finished his story and taken on a sadder air, bowed abruptly and left. I was ready to start hiking east at once, to catch up to Ducks and Brina and try with all my heart to make amends. Until someone's horse whinnied.

That shot my thoughts to Blind Thomas. I had to say good-bye to him. So, as antsy as I was to be traveling in the opposite direction, I backtracked to where the horses were penned. Luckily the place was emptied of humans; everyone was in Promontory, celebrating. I could say farewell in private.

Feeling a little sad, I climbed through the fence and quietly approached the lazing animals. Ears pricked at once and heads lifted, and when I murmured his name, Thomas nickered. I warmed. That was the first friendly greeting I'd gotten in days. Like the other horses, he was caked in dried mud. So when he lowered his head for a scratch, I dug my fingers into the grit and rubbed vigorously until the hairs gleamed. He groaned in pleasure.

What was going to happen to him? A lot of the horses were already being shipped away and sold for other work. But who would buy a blind horse? Any quick eye would mark him unfit for harness, though in truth he was as strong as any of the sighted horses, not to mention twice as dedicated. No, he'd end up at the slaughterhouse for sure.

I'd take him with me.

Somewhere, the saints were shaking their heads at how easily thievery had become a habit. But standing there with him, I suddenly felt that Blind Thomas was the one friend I still had in camp. He'd never been anything but faithful to me; I couldn't abandon him now.

Then reason demanded a listen. I couldn't just throw a halter on Blind Thomas and stroll off in broad daylight. He was railroad property, after all. What if someone reported us? That likelihood brought Mr. Strobridge looming into my mind, brandishing his pick handle. I'd better wait until dark.

The feed car offered ready shelter as well as a cushioned nest of empty gunnysacks. Having had no real sleep last night, I nodded off in minutes.

A chorus of impatient nickers nudged me awake. I

came to groggily, groping for my bearings. The fibrous bags felt nothing at all like my bunk. Where was I? Gaining my senses, I remembered the feed car and then realized that dusk had enveloped it and yet no one had fed the horses. They were whinnying in hunger. I climbed to my feet.

The instant they saw me, their calls multiplied. Excitedly they paced and jostled one another and kicked out. Except for Blind Thomas, poor creature, who stood off to one side swinging his head back and forth at this aggravating hiccup in his daily routine. The kid who was supposed to do the feeding was probably sprawled on his backside somewhere in Promontory, so I set to doling out the hay and the barley. While the horses ate, I filled a small bag with more barley and fastened it to my haversack. Then I placed a firm grip on my restiveness and waited some more. I sat in the door frame with my feet dangling, watching the stars come out and listening to the horses chewing. It felt like I was teetering on the edge of something big.

The sound of voices chased me inside the car.

"Hey, the horses have already been fed! I could have stayed in town."

"Well, no one's stopping us from going back. C'mon, let's try Conner's again. We're bound to draw better cards this time."

Silence returned after they left. I took a halter and rope and carried them through the night toward Blind Thomas's silhouette. My skin turned to gooseflesh because he was standing there in the dark waiting for me, his ears pricked, his sightless eyes focused on my approach. It was as if he knew my plans and was agreeing to them. He wanted to go with me. Feeling my heart swell against my ribs, I fitted the halter around his head, and we walked away from the railroad together.

Thirty-Four

We walked side by side for the better part of two hours, I suppose, before we came upon the first real settlement east of Promontory. Didn't need to see the town to know it sat just beyond that rocky knoll. Sodden manure and rotting garbage delivered an overwhelming stench, and a drifting cloud of smoke smudged the stars. Even standing this far out and well into the wee hours, I heard overloud voices soaked in whiskey that were continuing to celebrate the great achievement. It was one of those hell-on-wheels towns—variously named Murder Gulch or Deadfall or Last Chance—that sprang up alongside the rails. Now I was going to walk into one with a stolen horse and a sack of gold, searching for an inscrutable young Chinaman. Men were hung for less.

But I had to track down Ducks and Brina, and it was possible they were here, or maybe someone had seen them pass through. So Thomas and I, with ears cocked, cautiously made our way toward the rollicking outpost.

In minutes we were traveling down the muddy passage of a railroad camp trying to dress itself as a town. Dirt-stained tents sagged behind wooden false fronts cheaply constructed yet boasting of civilization's amenities: Yellow Bird Hotel, Lucie's Lunch Counter, Gundy's Emporium. Saloons and dance halls, however, outnumbered those businesses two to one, promising "unwatered whiskey," "Mexican monte," and "Madame Maggie's Dancing Girls." Horses, some saddled, a few hitched to wagons, waited patiently outside these establishments. Although tinny music and chatter spilled onto the murky street, one of the horses picked up the sound of Thomas's hooves and whinnied a welcome. Thomas, of course, immediately lifted his head and returned a loud, echoing reply. *Shh!* I pulled his head toward me to cover his muzzle, but our presence was known now, at least to the horses. We proceeded.

Sudden, harsh laughter burst from a saloon ahead, and some sort of commotion took over its entry. Dark figures wrestled with one another. Squawks and stifled cries punctuated the scuffle. A couple of the individuals broke free to come running through the night toward me: Chinamen. My presence startled them for a split second, deepening the fear on their faces, but they sprinted on past.

Rapid gunshots sent bullets whistling into the air; Blind Thomas snorted as one bullet came dangerously close. It pinged the rock-strewn ground and ricocheted in our direction. I jumped too and shortened his lead. We needed to get out of here, and fast, so I hurriedly guided him away from the tracks and into the charcoal-colored cloak of the desert. My heart banged so hard, my ribs hurt.

Maybe we should skip this town and just move on to the next one. But then a gun fired again, and this time it was followed by a dog barking. Blind Thomas lifted his head to listen, and I did the same. Could it be . . . ?

Men's coarse voices rose and fell. More heartless laughter soured the night. Something was still going on. The dog began barking with a fury. It *was* Brina!

I tugged Blind Thomas into a trot, and we went stumbling through the darkness, over rocks and scrub and back toward town. I was certain Brina was in the middle of big trouble.

Boldly, I trotted Thomas right along the center of the shadowy street to where the drunken men were now up to their mischief. There were fewer of them than before, it seemed, though it was hard to make out details in the thick night. The light filtering through the smoky windows of the saloon outlined three, or possibly four, men restraining another man in the street, outside the saloon's entrance. At their heels, Brina growled and snapped, so agitated that her feet lifted off the ground with each bark. Then someone booted her in the throat, and she tumbled into the mud with a strangled yelp.

"Hey! Stop that!" Dim faces turned in my direction. Something glinted, perhaps a gun, and I half froze, not certain what to do. Brina knew. She'd found her feet now and lunged at her attacker. His cry ripped the air as she savaged his leg, throwing her weight from side to side and snarling.

That brought a round of laughter. "Git him, dawg!" someone urged with the criminal's pleasure in brutality at anyone's expense.

I dropped Thomas's lead along with my haversack and ran toward them. Brina, with a vicious, teeth-bared grip on the man's leg, paused to catch her breath. But her shoulders hunched in place; her claws dug into the earth. She was determined not to give an inch.

The group shifted just enough that I saw the real cause of their entertainment: they held a struggling Chinaman in their midst, his arms pinned behind his back. The saloon's lamplight shone upon a long white petticoat that had been fastened around him. It was getting stretched and trampled as the man fought to free himself.

Ducks. I couldn't see his face, but I guessed it was him by his height and by the fact that Brina was so vehemently protesting his mistreatment. In the same bit of yellow light I saw that a man had yanked Ducks's braided pigtail from his neck and was preparing to cut if off with a knife. But at that instant Brina renewed her attack, heaving her weight backward with brute force and pulling her victim off his feet. That distracted the knife-wielding man for a moment, and I charged.

"Let him go!" I ran at him with all my might, but it was like slamming into a brick wall. He didn't budge, and somewhere I knew my pa was shaking his head. A fist clipped my jaw and sent me staggering backward.

What ye have to do, see, is wait. Always keeping yeerself at the ready. Always looking to deliver that one punch that decides everything.

Pulling myself tall and breathing hard, I heeded my pa's words and began sizing up the men. "Let him go," I demanded again, all the while observing. There were three of them. Brina had one on the ground for the moment. That left two. And two of us, counting Ducks and me. Even odds. Except for the gun, which was holstered for the moment.

"This ain't none of your business, boy," warned the man with the gun. He laid a hand on it.

"Let him go."

"Whaddya want with a dang coolie?" the one holding Ducks growled. "You that desperate for a sweetheart?"

The raucous noise from the saloon crackled in the air overhead and around me, but it seemed so distant all of a sudden that I got calm, oh, so calm. "Let. Him. Go." I made a fist and raised it in front of my face: a challenge. I made another one and held it in place: a defense.

"Oh, you're itching for a whupping, are ya?" And the one left off his gun to lumber into the street like an angry bear.

Wait, I cautioned myself. *Wait and watch.*

He swung wildly, and I sidestepped. He swung again, and I just managed to knock his fist away. I caught Ducks's eye and gave the nod, hoping he would get the message. He did. With a surprising burst of strength Ducks fought his way free of the man with the knife, spun around, and delivered a blinding fast jab. Then he turned and ran, having to hitch up the petticoat to gain speed.

That was my cue. Always be watching. Always be waiting. 'Cause you only got one knockout punch. Eyeing the roaring bully in front of me, I poured all my anger into my fist and knocked him into the mud.

Then I ran too, and Brina came bounding alongside.

Blind Thomas's huge silhouette loomed in the dark. The poor creature was prancing in sightless circles and snorting with worry. I scooped up my haversack and then reached for his dangling lead just as gunfire rang over our heads. He bolted. "Thomas!" I cried. "Whoa!"

Brina barked, and perhaps that made him hesitate a stride, because he slowed enough for a figure in white to come rushing toward him and snatch up the trailing rope. Thomas didn't even shy, and the two of them raced into the safety of the night with Brina and me right behind.

When the four of us were well down the tracks, out of sight of the town and out of breath, we took refuge inside the hollow of one of the railroad's abandoned quarries. Ducks ripped off the petticoat at once and kicked it aside. He ran his fingers along his braid, feeling for damage. That seemed to matter more to him than the fact that his face was scraped and bleeding. I could see the dark stain in the starlight.

I plopped onto a flat rock and tried to catch my breath. Brina shoved her face against my knee, panting but happy. "Hey, there, lass," I said. "You did yourself proud back there." She spun around to rub the other side of her face, and I checked her for injuries but found none. I did notice she was missing the leather collar I'd braided for her.

Ducks, holding on to Thomas's lead, found a seat for himself. He looked beaten down. "Thank you," he said softly, and I nodded, of course. He watched Brina continue to wriggle around me and slobber my hands and finally said, "You come for dog?" As if sensing she was the topic of discussion, Brina bounded over to him.

I shrugged, undecided. It hurt some to see Brina lavish such attention on him when she belonged to . . .

Well, maybe she'd never *belonged* to me. But I did like her. I did want her.

"No," I answered. And as our breathing grew more regular, I dug through my haversack and retrieved the stolen money bag. After weighing it a moment and considering what I was doing, I tossed it in Ducks's direction. It landed in the gravel halfway between us. *Thunk.* He looked at it but didn't say anything.

Minutes passed. Why didn't he just pick it up? What was he waiting for, an explanation? An apology? Brina trotted back over to me, stopping to sniff the money bag, and then, when she'd received some absentminded strokes, returned to Ducks. Behind him, Blind Thomas shook himself off and heaved a sigh. Cocking a hip, he prepared to doze. I tried to fill the space with words. "What are you doing out here?"

It was his turn to shrug.

"Mr. Chang said something about ancestors?"

Ducks shrugged again. He had every right to be closemouthed. Hadn't I tried to kill him?

I blurted out my apology. "I'm sorry about what happened back at camp, about those men tossing the nitro. I didn't think they'd do it."

He sat listening.

"I did try to stop them." My palms grew damp with sweat, even with the night's cold. This begging for forgiveness was uncomfortable work. "I just couldn't get it done in time. It wasn't my fault."

Brina chose that moment to sit herself down beside Ducks, which seemed an awful lot like she was choosing sides. Through the dark, she leveled her gaze on me, as solemn as a judge, waiting for more.

"I'm sorry for everything," I said at last. "Sorry for the way I treated you."

Ducks leveled his gaze on me, too, his smooth face impassive. Although I wasn't close enough to be certain, I suspected he looked upon me with the same weariness I'd noticed in Mr. Chang's eyes. He held his tongue the way Mr. Chang had, as well. What was left unsaid outweighed what was spoken.

Looking over at the trampled petticoat, I realized I'd clothed him in pretty much the same humiliation from the day we'd met. I felt low, awful low. I didn't know how I'd ever dig myself out of my own shame, and I stared down at my boots. The night's chill was starting to bite.

Ducks got up from his rock then, and I heard his boots and Blind Thomas's hooves crunch the sand as they walked over. Silently, he extended his hand and I recalled the same gesture I'd ignored long before. What a fool I'd been. This time I grasped his hand willingly.

He smiled that broad, generous smile that sloughed off life's injustices. "In my country say: Forget injuries; never forget kindnesses."

I didn't deserve that gift, but I accepted it. From a brother. "Thank you."

Thirty-Five

The morning sun in its pink sky illuminated a ragtag group if there ever was one: Keung (who'd asked me to use his given name) the daydreaming Celestial; his younger brother, me, an Irish thief; Brina, the hardy dog of questionable breed but unquestionable character; and Blind Thomas, the steady horse who saw none of our faults and lived but to give a good day's work.

"Where is family?" Keung asked, offering me a handful of chopped dried fruit that I didn't recognize.

"New York," I answered. The pieces felt spongy in my mouth but tasted okay. "A long way from here."

"You go there?"

I shrugged. "I don't know. My pa's dead." Ducks already knew that, but I kept talking, spilling my private worries. "He fought in the war with the Sixty-ninth, the Fighting Irish. I wanted to enlist, but he said I was too young, said I had to stay behind and take care of my ma and sisters and brother, so that's what I have to do now." I tugged my pockets inside out to show they were empty. "With all those mouths to feed I have to find work, and soon."

Both my conscience and my haversack were a lot lighter since I'd returned the gold coins to Keung. He'd finally accepted the money bag and admitted he'd had to work a year with no pay, getting food from his countrymen when he couldn't purchase it himself. I didn't understand how he could forgive me. "What about your family?" I asked. "Where are they?"

"No family. Uncle in Second City, you call Sacra—"

"Sacramento?"

"Yes. I no like his wife. She no like me."

"So you're not going back there?"

He shook his head.

The dawn paraded in silence. The sky turned from pink to pale blue, and as I gazed out across the valley I realized how pretty it was here. In the distance, hazy purple black mountains rose behind yellow gold hills that swept upward like ocean waves. Green and crimson grasses edged expanses of white salt flats that sparkled in the early sunshine. An angular flock of birds winged overhead, intent on their journey.

"So where are we going?" I asked.

"We?" He sat tall, like an overeager student. Brina,

who was curled nose to tail between us, lifted her head. Thomas was too busy with his breakfast of barley to pay any mind.

Okay. I gave in to a smile. His good humor was infectious. "Yes, we."

Keung looked in the direction of Promontory Summit. "No go back."

"The tracks go east, too." I indicated the rails marching across the valley floor toward those purple mountains.

"What is east?"

I shrugged again. "We don't know yet. Except for that miserable little place we visited last night, but we can give it, and others like it, a wide berth." He turned his face into the sunlight, and I saw that he was tumbling things over in his mind. "It's a big country," I added. "There's got to be something out there for us."

All the anger I'd been carrying since I'd come to work on the railroad had evaporated, whether from unleashing that punch or rescuing Keung or setting things right by returning his hard-earned gold coins and apologizing. It was a peaceful feeling I hoped I could hold on to for a long time.

"Mine for gold?" he asked.

I shook my head. "No, I've had enough of chasing after gold for a while. And enough winters in the mountains."

He thought some more. "Make . . . how you say . . . big garden? Grow—"

"You mean an orchard, a farm?"

"Yes." He moved his hands excitedly. "Can grow good foods, make soups, rice, can sell to many peoples." With his last gesture he indicated the great expanse of land around us and all the people the rails would be carrying into it.

"Hmm. Never thought of myself as a farmer. But we've got the workhorse, don't we now? And he's as good as any in harness."

"I good cook, too," he said, slapping his chest. "You see."

I remembered how often I'd envied the tantalizing smells coming from the Chinese camp. Others had too. Surely there'd be interest. And there would be hordes of people traveling right through this valley now that the transcontinental railway had been completed. But how much trouble would I be borrowing in partnering with a Chinaman? The world was quick to judge.

I gave the difficulties some serious consideration, then flicked them aside. Keung was more a friend to me than a foreigner. A brother rather than a Celestial. Besides, we weren't that different. Li was a Chinese name, after all: Malachy Gorm Li!

"We'd need to buy some land," I said.

Grinning, he lifted the bag of coins and jingled it.

"Fair enough." I offered my hand and he shook it. "Partners?"

"Partners."

"Well, the day is young. Let's see what we can find."

And so a rash journey that had begun under the stars only the night before continued at a more reasoned pace in the promising light of a new day. I didn't know what dangers lay ahead. I knew they'd arrive in some form, just as I felt confident we'd meet them head-on. Together. Shaking the dust off ourselves and squinting into the sunrise, the four of us—two kindred spirits, a horse, and a dog—set out, our hopes pinned on what lay on the horizon.

Author's Note

Some Perspective

Once, at a conference, I was asked if writers of historical fiction unfairly impose twenty-first-century ideals on their characters. In other words, is it fair to create a seventeenth-century girl who dreams of becoming a scientist, or a nineteenth-century slave who shakes hands with his owner?

Back then, I responded that my characters were always firmly entrenched in their culture, that they thought and behaved—however prejudiced or naive or cruel—as was typical for their time. That didn't make them bad people, just honest ones.

But honesty can make for uncomfortable reading. Case in point: the movement to remove ethnic slurs from Mark Twain's *Adventures of Huckleberry Finn*. Just how far should a publisher (or an author) retreat to make a story set in an unpleasant, yet important, point in history palatable to a modern audience?

In my research for this novel I learned that prejudicial opinions about Chinese immigrants (as well as Irish immigrants) eerily echo those today about Latinos and Arabs and basically any new immigrant group: *They're taking our jobs. They're ruining our economy. They're dirty. Drive them out.*

I open the newspaper to read about building a fence to keep Mexicans out of the United States and then, in the same paper, read about an archaeological dig uncovering a mass grave containing the bones of fifty-seven Irish immigrants, the reporter noting that "anti-Irish sentiment made 19th-century America a hostile place for the workers. . . ."

I was invited to attend a presentation by the Southern Poverty Law Center called "The State of Hate and Extremism in America." Owing to several factors, the speaker said, one being that "the color" of America is less white, racially motivated crimes are on a rapid rise. But wasn't this country founded on the belief that "all men are created equal" and that people possess "certain unalienable rights"?

So I have to admit that, as this book came into being, I did begin to develop an ulterior motive. I wanted my characters to stretch themselves beyond their mutual suspicions. I installed the ugly details to keep history accurate, but I also nudged the two men toward a tentative friendship. Was this unfairly imposing twenty-first-century ideals upon them? Possibly, though there are records of interracial partnerships and even marriages. I'd prefer to call it twenty-first-century hopefulness: an optimistic desire that we might take another look at, and learn something from, our history. Because those times hold up a mirror to our own.

Details, Details

Although *Tracks* is a work of fiction, many of the people and events portrayed in it are quite true. The temperamental Mr. Strobridge did lose an eye in a blasting mishap, as described. The corpulent Mr. Crocker did scheme to set the world track-laying record with the individually named Irishmen. A Christmas Day avalanche in 1866 did sweep away and kill several Chinese workers. Even the Maiden's Grave, a site tended by romantic railroad workers, exists in Nevada, though historians have since learned that Lucinda was not a young girl but a grandmother.

The mistreatment of the Chinese was all too real. Because they looked and dressed differently, they were ridiculed and alternately dismissed as feminine or less than human. One travel publication of the day placed them low on the evolutionary ladder, commenting, "Do not their caudal appendages and power of imitation show their relation to the monkey . . . ?" Whites certainly didn't want these oddities living anywhere near them, so the Chinese usually built their settlements in particular areas of towns, and on the railroad they erected tents a distance from the sleeping cars of the white railroad workers. Although the Chinese, the largest immigrant group in California, were required to pay a variety of taxes, they weren't allowed to vote, couldn't testify in court, and were denied citizenship, and their children were prohibited from attending public schools. Life only got worse once the railroad was completed. With a poor economy contributing to rising anti-Chinese sentiment, the US government enacted a series of laws that culminated in the Chinese Exclusion Act of 1882. That act expressly forbade Chinese individuals from entering the country and permanently separated families. It took over sixty years for the act to be repealed, though strict limits on Chinese immigration were kept in place.

Ducks's rituals are grounded in tradition and still practiced today, even those involving the star lovers Cowboy and Weaver Girl. After writing one of his scenes, I asked a Chinese-American friend and her mother to review it for accuracy. They subsequently began conversing animatedly in Mandarin; then my friend laughed and explained to me in English that she'd always wondered about the small jar of "special water" kept in the family cabinet. It turns out her own family has for years collected the Weaver Girl's tears in the form of curative rainwater. Ducks would smile.

A Note About Blind Thomas

The character Blind Thomas is based on a horse who may or may not have existed. According to several authors, a horse named Blind Tom hauled every rail laid by the Union Pacific Railroad, was hailed in the news-papers as a hero, and even appeared at the Golden Spike ceremony joining the tracks. But these authors have cited each other's books as proof of this legend-ary animal, and I've yet to find a primary source. The closest I've come is discovering a letter posted on an online museum and originally dated May 5, 1869, that describes the Union Pacific's team of laborers working near Promontory:

> Next come track liners who with bar get track in shape. These are aided by water carriers, back-iron men moving rail on cars, lad that picks up lost spikes, etc, and don't forget "Champion Tom," the horse pulling the cart of iron to the men, been with the crew since Omaha.

Whether this Champion Tom and the mythic Blind Tom are one and the same, I don't know. But I'd like to believe that such a noble horse existed, and I'm honoring that possibility with the character Blind Thomas in this book.

And in case anyone is wondering if a blind horse could actually be useful to a railroad, the answer is yes. Blindness does not necessarily keep horses from being ridden or driven. A few years after the transcontinental railroad was completed, a blind horse named Sleepy Tom, advertised as "the world's toughest piece of horseflesh," set a world record for pacing. And a few decades later, in the 1930s, a blind horse named Elmer Gantry actually gave jumping exhibitions with his rider. Blindness is nothing to great horses with bold hearts.

Blind Thomas also serves as a great metaphor for the single-minded determination that built this "greatest enterprise in the world." I'd like to think that his blindness allowed him to judge his caretakers not on their skin color but on their respective merits. As it should be.